AKINA, SACHEM'S DAUGHTER

By

Mildred E. Riley

Odyssey Books, Inc.
Silver Spring, MD

Published by
Odyssey Books, Inc.
9501 Monroe Street
Silver Spring, MD 20910

ISBN 1-878634-07-0

Published in the United States of America

October 1992

In loving memory of my parents,
James and Ethel.

PROLOGUE

Torremolinos — 1644

"You will lose your head! Have you gone mad?"

Ibraha glared at his friend, Khamseen, disbelieving what he had just heard. His breath came in explosive gasps that punctuated the noise of the coffeehouse.

Khamseen motioned to Ibraha to lower his voice, but his companion was dumbfounded by the news he had just received.

"Not even the most learned *Mohtasseh,* provost, could rescue you from such a foolhardy venture if you are caught."

The coffeehouse in the marketplace, or *souk,* was a general gathering place for the many traders and merchants who frequented it after a busy day's work. The room was blue from the smoke of the cigarettes and the favored pipes, called *hookahs,* that were being smoked. Raised voices of the men gesticulating, sharing and relating stories of their business day, resonated against the stone walls.

Outside in the dusty streets, sounds of vendors and camel drivers could be heard competing with the noise within.

Ibraha leaned closer to Khamseen, his mouth only a few inches from his friend's ear. "Tell me, why would you do such a foolish thing? 'Tis crazy enough to steal the emir's boat and try to cross a sea you know nothing about; but to take a strange girl you know nothing about... that you've just kidnapped from an Englishman on a whim... why, where are your brains?" Due to his consternation, Ibraha's dark skin flushed to a deep burgundy. "Khamseen, your foolhardiness will get you into a trap you cannot squirm out of! Your father told me more than once that he worried about your crazy, stubborn behavior."

"Only because I want more, Ibraha," Khamseen boasted. His handsome brown face was flushed with enthusiasm as he proposed his new adventure to his older friend. "I want to see more. I never even see the places my ships see! I build them, and someone else has the pleasure of sailing them. And I want to be rich, have more money someday, like the emir."

"Well, you won't do it by stealing the emir's boat, that's certain. You'll most likely die by his hand, that's what!"

Khamseen's father, Mustepha, and Ibraha often talked during the infrequent quiet times they had on the whaling vessel. Ibraha remembered how Mustepha had sighed when he spoke of his son's headstrong ways.

Now, Ibraha thought, *here is Khamseen asking me to join him in a venture that I know is foolish and I'm giving in to him, even though I know better.* He tried one more argument. *After all, I promised his father I'd keep an eye on him. He's almost like a brother to me.*

"And have you forgotten that you may be picked up

as a slave? You must know about the numbers of our people who have been captured and sold as slaves. It is dangerous to stray from familiar waters. Pirates and profiteers are all up and down the coast. Besides," Ibraha said, "I vowed after my last whaling trip to find a quiet life for myself. I want a wife and a family."

"Just this last time, Ibraha," Khamseen pleaded. He thought he saw a glimmer of surrender in his friend's eyes, so he pressed his case. "One last, great adventure before you leave the sea. You owe that to yourself. After all, you're only twenty-five, still a young man."

Khamseen wanted money and fame. The girl... well, that was something extra that made the adventure more exciting.

CHAPTER ONE

The blinding whiteness of the Spanish sun caused Akayna to squint her dark eyes into narrow slits to lessen its glare. Like brilliant shards of glass, the fiery orb threw flashing, blazing colors over the city's painted walls and cobblestones of the streets.

She threw back her head to free her scorching neck from the captured heat of her long, heavy, dark hair. Her leather clothing, comfortable in the woods of her home in Massachusetts, had rubbed her skin raw where it chafed her neck and arms. But even in her discomforting state, her beauty was evident. Her skimpy, bedraggled leather shift did little to disguise her loveliness. The tawny, reddish-golden hue of her skin seemed almost to radiate warmth and light. Thick raven hair framed her delicate face and fell like a silken waterfall to her slender waist. Her body, so delicately formed, appeared to have been molded and shaped by a fine artist's hand; she was like a fragile piece of sculpture. She held her lovely form with such nobility, that in the hubbub of her present surroundings she appeared ethereal.

She looked around her uncertainly. Was this England? Her destination; her haven?

That day, weeks ago, when Akayna had been accused of murder, seemed distant as she stood shaken, on foreign soil. Her friend, Ella Gardner, a neighboring settler's daughter, had been found dead in the field where the two girls had been gathering flowers. It seemed she had been struck by a boulder.

"I saw the rain clouds coming. I told Ella we should return home. She said she wanted to pick more of the sun daisies. When I reached Snake Road, I turned back and she was still picking more flowers," Akayna had explained to her father, Great Sachem Anesquam.

However, the settlers had insisted that Akayna must have pushed Ella, causing her to strike her head, thus causing her death, and she must pay.

Sachem Anesquam, concerned for his daughter's well-being, had immediately thought of his friend, Henry Kendall, the Crown's representative.

Akayna remembered how her father had told her about his life in a fishing village on the rocky coast of Maine — how he had learned to speak the white man's tongue. When he moved to Cape Cod to become chief of the Algonquins, he had greeted Captain Henry Kendall of the London joint stock company with, "Much welcome, white brother, much welcome!"

Peace treaties had been signed with Captain Kendall. So when the tragedy occurred, Sachem Anesquam rushed to him to seek his assistance.

"You must help my daughter," Sachem Anesquam had implored on that fateful day, reminding Henry Kendall of the fourth article of one of the treaties, which stated, *"If any did unjustly warre against him, we would ayde him; if any did warre against us, he should ayde us.*"

Since his wife's death, Akayna and her father had sought to comfort each other, and their relationship had deepened to replace the vacuum caused by their loss. Now it seemed like fate would separate them, too.

Kendall had agreed to help, though secretly he believed Akayna to be guilty of the crime. However, he had other motives. Henry Kendall was not able to succeed in England. With his cohorts, he had tried to make money from the colonization effort. He had failed in Virginia, but still he persevered. His mind raced. Here was an opportunity to make more money.

"Wal, Chief, I can take her to England like you say, but 'twill take more than a few coppers. A few hundred pounds, at least, I reckon."

The Chief did not hesitate in his response. "I have much wampum. Take all that you need."

Anesquam had been preached to by the missionaries and had become a "praying Indian." He pulled from his buckskin tunic a small Bible, a gift on his conversion. "You Christian man?" he asked Henry Kendall.

Kendall nodded, anxious to get the business completed. "Put your hand on book and swear to your God to protect Akayna, Peaceful One, from all harm and return her to her tribe."

"I swear," Kendall said as his mind raced far ahead of the time at hand. He would be rich this time when he returned to England. He would sell Akayna, along with the coffle of young men and cargo he had in the hold of his ship, *Morning Star.*

Henry Kendall was determined to return to England richer than he had left it. He wanted to move up in his class status, be one of the real new aristocracy, which would come about when he married Jocelynn, a magistrate's daughter. She had told him more than once, "I'll not marry a poor man, so come back a rich one, or do not come back at all."

Anesquam had no way of knowing that Henry Kendall had been transporting captives to Spain for sale. He knew that the sea captain traveled from the old world to the new one. He had heard that the sea captain had visited Roanoke Village until it failed, then had made his way north to Massachusetts to find more profitable ventures.

"Now," he said to Anesquam, "we best get her to the ship under the cover of darkness. 'Tis a good thing it's a black, moonless night, 'cause I think the patrols are out."

"Aye, I will bring Akayna to you. Will you cast off soon?"

"As soon as the lass is aboard."

Thoughts of her father's last words to her jogged deep in Akayna's memory. *"The Englishman has been paid well to keep you safe, protect you and return you to us unharmed, my daughter. When our enemies find the true one who did this crime, when all danger is past, I will send for your return. Never put far from your mind,"* he had added, *"you are Akayna, Peaceful One, beloved daughter and flower of Chief Sachem Anesquam."*

The captive sea that had held her in terror for the past several weeks still claimed her body as she tried to stand on uncertain legs. She could smell the brackish, nauseant odors that welled from the waters that reached the pilings.

The scent of overripe fruit from a nearby market

stall, and the pungent essence of roasted lamb seemed to overcome her and her mouth watered involuntarily. The heavy scents of the waterfront mixed together and rode heavily on the thin, flat air.

As she stood uncertain, bewildered, Akayna became aware of strange sounds. She wanted to cover her ears, but both hands were tied at her waist. She bent slightly, as if she could ward off the onslaught of noises — the brass gongs, braying mules, bellowing camels, and caravan drivers that exhorted their beasts of burden to move faster. She heard strange Muslim chants of Islamic worshipers, the shrieks and yells of children as they played around their parents' market stalls. Akayna, accustomed to more peaceful scenes, felt as if her nerve endings would sizzle and break. What strange place was this?

Henry Kendall pushed her forward brusquely as she stood on the wharf almost rooted in fear. From her father she had learned enough of the foreign tongue to recognize her present danger. Surely this place was not the England she had heard about?

"Move wench!" Henry Kendall's rough voice grated in Akayna's ears as she was jolted to her present plight. The coarse man jerked her forward, unmindful of the leather belt that had been tied around her waist.

"No pernt 'n draggin' yer feet! Nah," he spat a viscous blob of mucus at her feet. "'Tis the end of you 'n' me. Yer not a chief's daughter now, 'n' the few coppers yer pa giv' me to spirit ye out o' the country, I've got better uses fer. Now, mus' get a new owner fer ye." His brutal yank almost threw her off balance. She staggered.

He was quite anxious to finish his business of selling

his stolen property. He had noticed the colors of the union jack on one of the ships in the harbor. It reminded him of his home in England and the bride he had waiting there.

Looking at Akayna, he had some nagging regrets that he had not taken the opportunity to sample his attractive prize, but the *Morning Star* had been so crowded with captives — his own and those of the other slavers in this venture with him — he could scarcely find surcease for his sexual needs. He had tried once to fondle her when she was allowed on deck for a few minutes, but her screams and protestations could be heard by others; and not wanting to be seen as a failed conqueror, he made a sly, insulting remark and gave up. After weeks in the airless, suffocating confinement of the ship's bowels, the stench of unwashed bodies offered little appeal for intimacy. Nonetheless, Henry Kendall felt an insistent sexual arousal when he looked at his young captive.

Her eyes were wide with fear, but as dense and unfeeling as Kendall was, he could recognize the intelligence, yes, and the rebellion he saw in her deep set eyes. Oh, if only he had more time! 'Twould have been a pleasure to ravish one so young and lovely. It had been too long since he had felt the exquisite release of his sexual desire.

He shrugged as he pushed Akayna over the rough cobblestones of the market center.

A sea gull swooped effortlessly toward a wooden piling. Akayna saw it and wondered, *Will I ever feel that free again?*

CHAPTER TWO

Ibraha relished the feel of the ship's deck under his feet. This was where he was happiest. The sea winds that brushed across his dark skin were like caresses of a lover's tender touch. He loved it when the weather was warm enough so he could bare his chest to the hot sun as he stood at the wheel of a moving ship, making way over clear blue water. He had been only a boy when his feet first hit the wooden deck of a whaling vessel. It had been instant love, and now, fifteen years later, he had become first mate of a Basque whaling vessel.

Ibraha was a strikingly handsome black man. His ancestry included the Susu tribe, a group of people related to the Malinke of Guinea. Over six-feet-five-inches tall, Ibraha's Susu ancestry from Guinea, West Africa, gave a blackness to his supple, glowing skin that seemed almost carved in its smoothness. His father's family were centered around Conakry, the seaport capital. Portuguese, French and English had all competed for trade along the Guinea coast, and as a boy Ibraha became familiar with those languages.

Living so close to the sea, he had learned to be a strong swimmer, and often dived from the occasional rocky outcrops into the ocean. His hard, muscled body bore testimony to his healthy vigor. His upper body, strengthened by his years as a whale harpooner, was defined by crisp delineations of well-formed muscles. His face, a compromise between his African father and his Basque mother, could be stern and arrogant, or gentle and appealing, depending on his mood or situation.

His friends trusted him with their lives, his enemies feared him. They knew if they thwarted him, his black eyes would turn to ice and his anger could almost devour them. But Ibraha reckoned with his volatility, and only when pushed did he allow his darker disposition to show. He preferred a peaceful existence and he always endeavored to find it. His great size was tempered by his calm manner and his desire for peace. Gentle by nature, nonetheless, he could be fierce if provoked.

He had met deep sorrow as a young child. When the Portuguese began trading in slaves, Ibraha's father had fled his homeland on a French ship loaded with palm oil, hides and peanuts. He swam ashore one dark night when the ship docked in Gibraltar, and he made his way along the coast to the port city of Torremolinos. He apprenticed himself to a lapidary who taught him how to cut, polish and engrave precious stones. Eventually he married, and soon after, Ibraha was born.

Ibraha lived a happy life until his mother, a daughter of a Torremolinos fisherman, became ill. His aunt had found him crying that day almost fifteen years ago. He had run mindlessly from his mother's deathbed, out of the house and down the thick, white-walled steps to the sea. When Ibraha's father saw his beautiful wife unable to eat, despite his pleas, and fail before his eyes, he couldn't bear it. One rose-colored evening, he simply walked into the deep waters of the Bay. The day his body washed ashore was the same day Ibraha's young mother died.

"O, Nino!" his aunt cried as she gathered the small, thin, weeping boy in her arms. That day Ibraha vowed he would never love another human being. It was too painful when one lost them. Ibraha remembered his first taste of whaling. His aunt's husband, who was a Basque fisherman, decided to take the lad back to sea with him.

"What else is there for him?" he asked his wife. "He cannot stay here in Torremolinos and remain idle. If he goes with me, at least he'll learn a trade."

"But what can he, a boy of ten, do?"

"We can find many things for him to do."

"But he'll be in the way, underfoot, and who knows in what kind of danger. Besides, you'll be gone for months! And," she anguished, "he's all I have left of my sister."

"Woman! Let the boy have a chance to grow! If I know you, you will only make a pet out of him. He deserves a chance to become a man."

Ibraha's uncle had never put much stock in his brother-in-law's business. Making jewelry, rings, earrings and bracelets, eh — what kind of trade was that? No, he'd take the boy with him. He'd learn soon enough how to become a man, live on the ocean, hunt and kill the leviathans of the sea, and most of all, meet the winds of change head-on as they came into his life.

Ibraha's uncle, Korous, was proud of his wife's nephew. Tall, almost six-feet-five-inches, Ibraha carried himself with head erect. His wide, strong shoulders and neck supported a noble head. His face, skin bronzed almost to a dark mahogany-black, added to his handsome appearance. Sooty-black eyebrows deepened the shadows of his mineral coal eyes. His was not a harsh face, but one weathered and softened by the winds and waters of the ocean. Those close to him were taken in by the welcoming warmth of his smile. His uncle loved him like the son he never had.

Early that summer evening his uncle Korous had joined Ibraha on deck. The whaling vessel had been secured and unloading would commence early the next morning. The barrels of whale oil, bundles of baleen and whalebone, as well as crates of salted meat, would be taken ashore to be sold in the marketplace. "Do you think Tante will soon be down to greet us, Uncle Korous?" Ibraha asked.

"Nothing would keep her away once she knows you are here," his uncle said, smiling.

The familiar noises of the harbor echoed around them as they sat on the deck of the gently swaying ship.

"Look, Uncle," Ibraha pointed to a scruffy looking ship anchored a hundred yards from where they were anchored. "Isn't that the ship *Morning Star* we saw when we passed through the Straits of Gibraltar a few days back?"

"Aye, I remember when I trained my glass on it, I think I saw human cargo."

Ibraha shook his head with dismay. He felt sorrow and pity for anyone confined, and on such a poorly maintained vessel. He moved aside as Mustepha, the older harpooner who had taught him the singular technique of harpooning a whale, came and sat on a coil of ropes nearby. The three men sat in comfortable silence, each enveloped in his own thoughts.

Mustepha's grayish sparse beard, that framed his brown leathery face, bobbled as he cleared his throat before he spoke. "I'm anxious to see my son Khamseen and find out if he has finished the emir's boat. When we left here some months ago he had just laid the keel. Should be near done by now."

"Aye," Ibraha's uncle agreed. "He is a clever builder, that son of yours. You must be proud of him."

"That I am. I think I will stay ashore with him for a time. I want to spend some time with him. Not getting any younger..."

"Who is?" Korous smiled at his old friend. "I feel as if I have only a trip or two left in my old bones. But this one," he slapped Ibraha playfully on the back, "this one has many, many ocean trips ahead of him, eh, lad?"

Ibraha nodded wordlessly. His mind was on the ship. "Human cargo," his Uncle Korous had said.

He glanced toward the *Morning Star*. She was an ungainly looking packet, rigged fore and aft. Her sails were dingy and drooping, as if no one cared. Some of her lines were carelessly draped, not tied securely to the mooring posts, and the ship wobbled restlessly in the water.

Ibraha wondered what kind of unfeeling captain would allow such slovenliness. Sighing, he took his spyglass and examined the hapless vessel. He could see a group of red-skinned men with long black hair huddled at the stern of the ship. They seemed to be tied together. *Poor devils*, he thought. He was just about to lower the glass when he heard a woman's scream. The shrill, piercing cry reverberated over the quiet harbor waters like the shriek of a wounded bird. He moved his eyepiece in the direction of the sound. And he saw Akayna.

Framed in the circle of the glass was the loveliest face he had ever seen. He turned the focus to bring the vision closer into view. Hair like luxurious black silk framed a face of reddish-gold coloring. Dark eyes, wide with apprehension, were framed by black fringes of curling eyelashes. Even from the distance between them Ibraha sensed a presence about her that spelled self-awareness.

Slowly he moved the spyglass down the slender lines of the lovely creature's body, taking in the finely molded arms and legs. Where had this being come from and where was she going? Would he ever see her again?

As he lowered the glass slowly, he realized that he had been holding his breath while he looked at her. He would have to find her.

CHAPTER THREE

England was in turmoil. And so was the household of Sir Lawrence Stuart. His son, Sir Aidan, disagreed with his father about the recent turn of events in the country's government. "Sire, for more than ten years the king has tried to rule England without a Parliament. He is bound to fail. Surely you know that."

"I do not know that!" his father protested. "I know that he has tried to call one Parliament after the other, only to be met by dunderheads who do not understand that the king must have absolute power!"

"Father!" Sir Aidan said impatiently, "Charles the First said he would accept the Petition of Rights! Then he changed his mind, saying if those provisions were permitted they would make absolute government impossible. He can't keep denying the will of the people."

Sir Aidan saw his father's face flush with anger as Sir Lawrence sat down abruptly in his chair behind his massive desk. He looked at his son and spoke slowly, with assurance.

"They are just a horde of Puritans, against the Crown and the church. And I don't understand why I have a son who dares agree with their principles.

"It's a matter of conscience, father. You taught me that. I, for one, cannot live in a country that would banish clergy with Puritan leanings, or that will censor the press and suppress religious meetings except those of the high Anglican church. What kind of life are we going to have here?"

His father sighed and looked directly at his son. "We will have an England that we have always had, with a king to lead us, as before."

"It will fail, father. Absolute power without financial backing will fail. And the people are not ready to offer that financial support. There are too few, and they are not prepared to lose so much. I know you don't want to hear me say this, father, but I oppose the king."

"What you say is treason!" Sir Lawrence slapped both hands on his desk and glared at his son who stood before him. "Don't you know that?" he demanded.

Indeed, Sir Aidan did, and in 1642, when the crisis came, the Parliament and the nation had to choose. King Charles tried to arrest five members of Parliament who had been recognized as leaders of the opposition. Sir Aidan was one of them.

He barely escaped arrest. Undercover and in disguise as a merchant, and accompanied by his wife, he was able to flee the country, finally landing in Torremolinos.

His young wife, Anne, was so upset by the sudden change in her life from a pampered member of British aristocracy to almost exile in a small Spanish town, that she began at once to refuse all social contact with her husband. She isolated herself most of the day in her suite of rooms and joined her husband only for the evening meal. She was gracious, charming and witty, behaving much as she would to a special dinner guest.

Sir Aidan knew she was unhappy, and he regretted the abrupt change in their lives.

"Anne, you know how much I love you. Please let us get on with our lives!" he begged her more than once.

His plea fell on deaf ears. Almost two years had gone by. His wife seemed lovelier to him than the day they had married, but the distance between them grew wider. They were two strangers living in the same house.

The only comfort either had was the presence of the indentured servant, Mistress Cooley, who had been Sir Aidan's nursemaid. Although he had offered her freedom upon his hasty flight from England, she had refused.

"Wot 'twould it do fer me, now?" she asked him. "Nah, ah've lived wid ye all me life, 'n' to leave yer household now, 'twould be foolish. Best fer me to die 'n yer service." She continued anxiously, "Ye'll still be needin' me, won' cher, sir? "Aye, Mistress Cooley. And glad I am that you are with Lady Anne and me." He smiled at the short, stocky, middle-aged woman.

Mistress Cooley was aware of the tension between Sir Aidan and his wife. She agonized over the situation, but knew she could do little about it. She wasn't even certain if Sir Aidan knew, but she was aware of the empty sherry bottles that were culled each morning from her lady's wastebasket. If only there were children. Well... she'd "do" for Sir Aidan as long as he needed her. He was all the family she had, the surrogate son she knew she could not abandon.

She was stunned when he told her, "I'll be bringing a young woman into the household. She is to help with any duties you may give her, and hopefully assist Lady Anne, as a personal maid."

"Indeed, sir, as you wish, sir." Mistress Cooley dipped a little curtsy to her employer. *Wot does 'e need another woman in this 'ouse fer?* Then her face flushed as she thought of the two separate lives being lived under her own nose. She could not approve or disapprove of such goings-on, so she kept her ideas to herself.

• • •

As he picked his way toward the center of the market, Sir Aidan saw a small group, isolated to one side. He noticed a ruddy-faced man whom he judged to be English trying to manage a coffle of what appeared to be Indians. Their burnished red-brown skin and straight black hair indicated that they were a race of people not usually seen in this part of Spain. A small, curious crowd had gathered around them. As he neared the group, some of the onlookers parted, aware of the presence of the well-to-do Englishman.

Then Aidan saw Akayna. He noticed that she held her head erect, as if to meet any challenge. He observed her exquisite form despite her tattered, soiled leather shift. She stood out like a flawless jewel beside the unkempt Indian men. Her singular beauty seemed to separate her from the others.

He could see that she was aware of him as well. She watched as he came closer to her. Her deep set eyes never wavered as she saw him approach. She had seen his kind before. She realized that he was an Englishman, dressed as he was in silk pantaloons, white stockings, black buckled shoes, and a brass buttoned jacket that was sashed with a wide swath of colored cloth. His hat was black velvet, festooned with a white ostrich feather. Sir Aidan doffed it as he came nearer to make an inquiry of the anxious Henry Kendall, who told him he wanted twenty-five pounds for the girl alone.

Akayna raised her chin defiantly as she watched the transaction take place. She endeavored to pull her arms closer to her body as if to strengthen herself. As the two men concluded their business, she watched warily as they came closer. She saw a knife in Henry Kendall's hand. Did he intend to kill her?

She screamed, and Henry Kendall clapped his grubby hand over her mouth as he cut the leather bindings from her waist.

"No! No!" she yelled out as she tried to run. "England! England! Must go to England. This not England!"

Sir Aidan was dumbfounded to hear the girl speak of his homeland. What did she mean? What did she know of England? This Indian girl?

Henry Kendall grabbed the struggling girl by her long hair and swung her face around toward his own.

"We'll hev none o' that! Yer not in the new world now, me pretty, but in the ol' one, where things are done different. 'Tis this fine gentleman," he nodded toward Sir Aidan, who wondered if he would get this spitfire back to his villa, "he's the one who owns ye now." Henry Kendall continued to wrestle with the struggling girl.

"Perhaps," Sir Aidan intervened, anxious to lessen the commotion, "perhaps it would be better to keep the shackles on her."

He motioned to his coachman who stood waiting beside the cabriolet. The two men, Kendall and the coachman, struggled to drag the resisting young woman to the vehicle. She was thrown onto the horsehair seat cushion and her hands were tied to the railing of the coach. Sir Aidan instructed his driver, "To the villa, as quickly as you can."

CHAPTER FOUR

Khamseen, the young African boat builder, happened to be at the marketplace when he saw the exchange of the Indian girl take place. Accustomed to the hubbub and excitement that usually occurred at the busy place, he might not have paid any attention, except that he saw Akayna. He was stunned by her beauty. His eyes were drawn to her tawny, red-brown coloring, her slender body, and he saw her shake her head, her blue-black hair moving violently as she screamed, "No! No!"

As Khamseen watched, her eyes caught his and he saw in the look the unmistakable terror of a trapped animal. He saw stark fear as her eyes locked momentarily on his.

Akayna's eyes were indeed on the tall black man as he moved nearer to her. This strange looking person — did his blackness mean he was painted for war? Was he going to attack them?

His black eyes, which seemed to pull her right into them, were almost hidden beneath dark, heavy eyebrows. His nose was straight and gave his face a clean, open look. He was solemn, but as he approached the buggy that she had been tied into, she could see that his was not a hard mouth, but one that appeared to have signs of interest in her.

Akayna struggled to bring her body into a more dignified position, but the leather strap around her waist had been so tightly anchored, she felt as helpless as a trussed animal.

Whatever hope she had died as she watched the black man walk by, seemingly unconcerned about her plight. She did not realize that on his way to conduct his business, Khamseen had taken particular notice of Sir Aidan and his carriage. He would recognize it when he saw it again.

He continued on his way to the brass stall where he intended to purchase more brass fittings for the ship he was building. The *Sea Treasure* was a beautiful vessel and Khamseen had been commissioned by a wealthy emir to design, build and outfit her for his use. No expense had been spared by Khamseen in preparing the vessel. He hoped that the emir would not be adverse to paying the sum he would charge for his labor.

Mahogany lined the ship's cabin walls; teak wood floors in the salon forward, with brass railings for safety on the wall perimeter, contributed to its elegance and safety. Brass fittings and soft Moroccan leather had been used throughout the interior. In the galley special compartments had been built to hold cutlery, Spanish ceramic dishes, plates, cups and glassware. Cooking utensils of copper and iron hung on walls over the cooking area. There was a bathroom with a tiled stall for bathing, and a commode was also tiled with blue glazes. This lent a clean serenity to the tiny alcove. No space had been wasted; every object, every utensil, had its own use and its own space.

Khamseen was proud of his work and the work of his craftsmen. His greatest desire was to own and navigate a ship like the *Sea Treasure.* He, like others, had heard much about the new world. He and his father, Mustepha, had dreamed of making the voyage. Others — Spanish, Italian, and Portuguese — had done so; why not an African sailor?

Khamseen thought, to give up the *Sea Treasure* would be losing a part of himself. More than anything, too, he wanted to be with her on her maiden voyage. He did not know, at the time, that he would steal her.

• • •

"By God, 'n' where did ye fin' this one?" Mistress Cooley asked the coachman when he half-dragged, half-carried the resisting Akayna into the back corridor of the villa. She observed the pubescent, budding body of Akayna, as well as the straps and ties that bound her. "She's used to walkin' barefoot, that I can tell ye. Where did Sir Aidan get her?"

The coachman stood rubbing his hands together as if Akayna's skin color had stained them. "A place beyond beyond," he replied. "The slaver at the market said she is called Indian, but to tell ye the truth, I'd never seen her like when I was in Karachi some time back." He backed away from the trussed up girl.

Akayna stared at the two. Although they spoke quickly and with a strange accent to her ears, she understood the words "Indian" and "slaver." She had decided that perhaps her salvation lay in maintaining an impassive attitude. She would give them no inkling of what her inner thoughts or plans for escape might be. Often her father had counseled, *"The Algonquin way means always be true to one's self. Find inner strength to overcome your enemies. Remember that our great Sachem, Assawon, Commander in Chief of our tribe, never camped in the same camp, or in the same place, twice. A great Wampanoag Sachem, he kept his enemy confused. He did not speak what was in his heart."*

If she could confuse these people, if she could look deep into her own spirit, somehow, someway, she would return to her father's home; their *wikiyapi*, their frame hut covered with bark, brush and matting in the center of the village. It was home. If she closed her eyes she could see the everlasting flame of the family hearth, the soft luxurious furs that were placed at evening time on fresh boughs of wood for comfortable, warm sleeping beds. She could almost hear the call of the bobwhite, the killdeer's trilling voice and the noisy woodpecker throbbing with his bill as he searched for grub beneath the tree bark. Home to her was so many things, she felt she would have to find a space in her memory to secrete them all for safekeeping so they would not be lost to her. She would need the memories to sustain her life and keep her as Akayna, the Peaceful One, flower of Anesquam, great Sachem.

On the other hand, Mistress Cooley, being a practical soul, began to take charge and give orders. "The furst thing is a good cleanin' up. All over, 'specially the hair. Like as not, 'tis filled with vermin."

She turned to the coachman and ordered, "Tell the kitchen girl to get in here quick. We'll bathe her here in the corridor so as not to take anythin' bad into the house proper."

The kitchen girl, a young Moroccan, dragged out a round brass tub. She returned with two buckets of warm water which she poured into the tub.

Still tied and hobbled, Akayna watched with apprehension. What was the round thing that looked like a cookpot? She had always bathed in the stream behind the village. She steeled herself to hide her fear.

Mistress Cooley saw the distancing in the young Indian girl's eyes and she felt the almost palpable serenity the girl exuded, but she shook her head and decided to get on with her assignment. Sir Aidan was the type of man that wanted his orders carried out promptly and efficiently. She'd better have the girl presentable by the dinner hour.

She pushed a wooden screen around the tub for privacy and approached Akayna.

A robust, motherly woman with soft blue eyes, she touched the girl gently. "Now, 'twill make ye feel better," she said softly, rubbing her hand with long, quiet strokes along Akayna's arm as if trying to calm her, "if ye gets a good bath 'n' cleanin' up. Cum now, into the warm water."

She loosened the straps and pulled the leather shift over Akayna's head, kicking them along the floor to the kitchen girl. "Burn them," she instructed. "She'll not need them again."

The soothing water, and the sensitive warmth she felt from Mistress Cooley, calmed Akayna. She submitted to the soaping, the lathering and scrubbing with no sign of the inner anxiety she felt. Mistress Cooley lathered and washed Akayna's blue-black hair, then wrapped a coarse cloth around the slender figure as she assisted her out of the tub.

As the woman busied herself with toweling and drying Akayna's hair, she remarked, almost to herself,

"'Tis truly a crownin' glory. Raven black and thick. Smooth as silk, it is, too."

As she worked, she kept up a steady stream of chatter. Some of the words were new to Akayna, but others she understood. She understood that Sir Aidan was the man who had purchased her.

"Ye could do wurs' then hev' Sir Aidan as yer benefactor," she said.

Akayna wondered what did she mean, "benefactor?" She watched as Mistress Cooley pulled a pair of white pantaloons from a pile of garments and indicated that Akayna was to step into them. Then she made Akayna raise her arms for a white cotton shift which fell much too long around her ankles.

"Ah, well," she sighed, "hev' to tie it up with a bit o' ribbon for now."

She kept up her chatter. "Nah, I know 'tis strange, the whole idea to a gel like yerself in a strange land 'n' strange place, but ye mus' learn to mek do, if needs be, do widout; sometimes 'tis all a body kin do to stay alive."

The woman jerked a peach-colored silk and muslin gown over Akayna's head. Her beauty stunned Mistress Cooley as she saw the effect of her handiwork. Unaccustomed to seeing people with Akayna's coloring, she noticed how Akayna's skin tone was enhanced by the soft blooming color of the gown. Akayna's black-locked hair, and midnight eyes fringed with long sooty eyelashes, astonished the servant.

Unaware of her striking looks, Akayna's mind reeled with the turn of events as she took note of her surroundings. She could see over Mistress Cooley's shoulder, beyond the doorway into a sunny open courtyard.

Lemon trees, jeweled with ripening fruit that nestled against glossy green leaves, formed an inviting pathway that led to the garden.

As Mistress Cooley continued to fuss over her, turning her this way and that, Akayna sought sanctuary in the deep recesses of her mind. *Why did this bad thing happen to me? Oh, Manitou, Great Spirit,* she prayed, reverting to her childhood deity, *please take me back to my father. I have not harmed any of your creatures. Do I deserve to be abandoned?*

"Mistress Cooley?" Akayna had heard the coachman address the woman that way. She spoke aloud for the first time since her arrival at the villa. Her voice was low and throaty, and the servant was startled at the sound of English from the Indian girl.

She paused in her work. " 'Tis me, child, tryin' me best to fit yer fer Sir Aidan."

"Fit me? What is 'fit me'?"

Mistress Cooley placed her hands on Akayna's shoulders for a moment, then spoke sympathetically to her. She continued to pin and tuck the gown to Akayna's slim figure. "Wal, almos' me whole life has been takin' keer o' Sir Aidan, ye might say, an' now that means gettin' ye ready."

"Ready?"

"Aye, ready to sit at the dinner table tonight."

"I do not know about such things." Akayna threw back her head and shook her hair in a black cloud of denial. "I must return to my home. I do not belong here. My father sent me to England for safety. If this is not England, I must go home." She stared at Mistress Cooley, as if willing the woman to obey her.

Through years of servitude, Mistress Cooley had

learned when to speak and when not to speak. She knew it was best to ignore Akayna's plea since she could do little about it; however, she did feel a stab of empathy.

With pins in her mouth, she moaned in dismay as she continued to adjust the gown. "There now, me thinks if yer don' twist about too much, 'twill do fer tonight. Now that I've seen yer size, I kin fix up the rest o' the gowns 'n' undergarments. Mayhap the kid shoes'll be a mite big, but yer won't be walkin' too much tonight."

Akayna was led into a small salon off the kitchen area. As she passed by the area, she glimpsed huge brass pots hanging on the walls, as well as iron cooking cauldrons resting on the floor near the hearth. The stone floors felt strange to her poorly shod feet, and she shuffled awkwardly as Mistress Cooley led her to a dressing table with a small mirror on it.

"We'll do yer hair now," she said.

The woman began to brush her hair. It fairly crackled as the coarse bristles smoothed and straightened the silky entanglements. Soon the black cloud was transformed into an attractive halo — thick braids intertwined with slender peach-colored satin ribbons.

"'Twill be a strange turn o' events when Lady Anne sees yer, I'm thinking," Mistress Cooley cackled half to herself. "There now, 'tis a new self ye see, eh?" She turned Akayna to face the mirror.

For a moment Akayna was confused. She did not recognize her image at first. The reflection was not the one she was accustomed to seeing in the bathing stream behind the village. Who was the person in the mirror?

She saw a red-gold hued face with startling planes cast by high cheekbones. Slightly slanted large, dark eyes indicated a sad, sorrowful, lonely person, but her straight nose, gently flared at the nostrils, gave her an elegant look. Her mouth, with soft lips that curved slightly, revealed none of the tension she felt.

Akayna closed her eyes and dropped her face into her hands. Her reaction was not expected by the woman. "I do not know her; Akayna is no more," she muttered between her fingers. "Akayna has gone from the earth."

"Akayna's yer name, eh? Nonsense, 'tis a beauty ye are! Ye'd turn the head of any man now that yer not in yer native clothes. With yer golden color, Sir Aidan's goin' to hev' 'is 'ands filled or my name is not Mistress Amylyne Cooley!"

CHAPTER FIVE

Torremolinos, a small coastal town situated on the Mediterranean sea, made its living on the commercial fishing activities in its blue-green waters. The town proper consisted of a few dusty streets with some small shops and eating places. Beyond the streets, that were fronted by the wharf, was the main square, with Saint Domingo's church and bell tower as its dominant features.

The few residences of any note were stretched out farther beyond the square. Each had its own cluster of smaller houses, forming intimate family compounds.

Khamseen, armed with information he had gained in discreet questioning of the natives concerning Sir Aidan, had no difficulty locating the Stuart household. About ten miles from the town proper in the foothills of the mountains, Sir Aidan lived in a villa with a central main structure. There was an indoor patio, inside and outside corridors, a two-story section called the pavilion, and a smaller, two-story carriage house, with stables below the living quarters for the servants above.

A handsome sweep of the veranda, supported by heavy columns over paved brick flooring, shaded and cooled the inner rooms on the first floor. The gardens of the house were located around the house proper.

Khamseen moved on silent feet as he made his way past the veranda and peered through the long open windows. It was close to evening; dusk had descended and it was near the dinner hour. Khamseen's sense of smell was piqued by the scent of the lemon trees that bound the inner courtyard.

As he moved quietly about, checking for any obstacles he might encounter, his mind returned to the afternoon. If he could rescue her, surely out of gratitude she would be his. He would have an exotic creature like no other in all of Torremolinos. That would certainly increase his stature among his friends. There was nothing wrong with that.

He could imagine her slipping into his arms, her raven-dark hair secreting them into an embrace that would exclude the world. He had never seen a more lovely creature. He could almost taste the sweetness of her soft lips yielding under his firm mouth. How could he make such things come to pass? He, a mere African shipbuilder, with his only resources his hands and his brains. But he would succeed, he vowed, as with any other undertaking he had planned.

What he had heard on the waterfront, from the talk of the burly seamen that loitered about the barrooms and docks, was that Sir Aidan Stuart had at last found someone to serve as his mistress. It turned Khamseen's stomach to think that one so innocent should be caught up in such a despicable set of circumstances. The fact that his own motivation for seizing her was a little less honorable did not enter his mind.

He walked the perimeter of the compound, surprised

there were no guards or dogs to set up alarms. He noticed lights from candles scattered about in several of the rooms. He saw no activity. Was everyone already in bed? Were the occupants in a main room for dinner? Was the Indian girl still trussed up like an animal?

He decided to leave and return at midnight. He had to find her. He remembered the look that had passed between them that afternoon. The message communicated between them came as clearly as if the words had been spoken. Hers pleaded for help; his said, "Fate sent you to me." He did not doubt for a moment that she could not be used to help him reach his personal goals — financial success, and an elevated social status. Even the emir did not have such an alluring creature in his harem.

• • •

Boats of all types, shapes and construction, from ark-like conveyances to dhows, fishing dorys, sailing craft of every description, as well as brigantines and full-rigged vessels filled the harbor. Ignoring them, Khamseen made his way to the pier farthest from the center.

He walked lightly, his body straight and lithe, all six-feet-four-inches, supporting supple muscles and long bones. His broad shoulders almost filled the hatchway and he had to stoop to enter his houseboat, a makeshift place he called home. He planned to eat quickly and prepare for his midnight venture.

Thinking of the loveliness of the Indian girl as he prepared his meal, brought to mind vague images of his mother. Khamseen remembered little of his mother. He had been very young when she died and the only real memory of her that he had was the cool smoothness of her voluminous *chadah* as she held him in her lap, telling him stories of her life in the African desert. She had been the daughter of an African nomad. Her father sold brass articles and leather goods made by the craftsmen of their tribe.

Khamseen's father was a Moroccan fisherman who traveled great distances along the North African coast in the fishing trade. He once told Khamseen, "Your mother was such a beautiful woman; soft like the zephyr winds of early summer, and as gentle as a flower awakening to the sun. And how I loved her! Her black eyes were so deep, like yours, my son, I could almost drown myself in them. Even her name was beautiful. Lydia."

"How did you meet mother?" Khamseen had asked.

His father, a swarthy, bronzed man, his skin leathered and wrinkled by exposure to the sun and water, would pull on his *hookah*. He would draw a cloud of smoke from the water pipe before he would answer.

"It was at a bazaar. I was looking for new ropes and sails for my boat. I had almost decided to return home and continue looking another day, when I stopped at her father's stall. He sold leather and I wanted some to patch my water skins that I used when I went out to sea."

"And, and," young Khamseen, who knew the story well, but delighted in hearing it often, would ask.

"And there she was. A tiny, gentle creature with skin like black satin; smooth, pure, with not one blemish or mark. None, I tell you, on her entire body. She was like a marble statue, except she was warm and soft. Her eyes were beautiful, and her lips! — I tell you, child of my loins, her lips were like the ripest of sweet pink melons.

And when she smiled," his father said with remembered passion, "when she smiled, it was as if the heavens opened and said, 'Welcome, love.' I thought she was the most beautiful creature ever put on the earth. One day, may you find a woman as near like your mother as possible."

The old man had settled back on his cushions to continue smoking. The sweetish smoke from the *hookah* formed a gentle halo around his graying head.

Khamseen remembered the stories as a link to his African and Moroccan heritage. He wanted more, however, for himself.

CHAPTER SIX

Later that night, alone in the bedroom assigned to her, Akayna looked around. A single bed with a frothy lace coverlet had been turned back for her. The stucco walls, sand-colored, were bare except for a niche carved into one wall. It contained a small clay figure, like a doll, Akayna thought. Iron grillwork covered the window on the east wall. On a small table rested a candle and its snuffer.

A chest at the foot of the bed was covered with a soft rug. Akayna felt closed in and imprisoned in the tiny room. She had come so far from home and so much had happened to her.

Still in shock, she sat on the floor and faced the window. She wanted to pray. She crossed her legs and placed her hands on her knees, palms turned upward in supplication. She raised her face toward the open window. She had released her hair from Mistress Cooley's design, and her two long familiar braids fell over her breasts. She prayed to the *Manitou* she loved best.

Oh, Kautantowwit, God of the southwest wind, your daughter, Akayna, begs for your help. Do you know of my innocence? Can you not feel the grief of my being?

Can you hear me in this strange land? she sobbed. *Will I ever return to my father's wetu?* A picture of her father's home came into her mind. It was fuzzy and indistinct. She realized that somehow it was becoming more difficult to bring the picture into focus. Everything in this "old world" was so strange to her.

As she peered through the grillwork of the window, she could see the small crescent of the evening moon low on the horizon. Her heart sank. It was an ill omen. The crescent moon standing almost on its end meant the "night-sun," as the Indians called it, was emptying itself and would spill only bad luck and trouble to the people below.

Akayna's eyes filled with tears. What else could go wrong? As she peered through the darkness, she thought she saw something. She blinked her eyes rapidly to stop her tears and tried to focus them. A slight movement caught her attention. A bright yellow feather drifted slowly from the window to the floor. Akayna watched it in amazement as it came to rest near where she prayed. Where had it come from; was there a bird clinging to the vines outside the window?

She stood closer to the window. She saw nothing, heard only the heavy silence of the night. She studied the delicate feather she held in her hand. There had to be a message there for her. Perhaps from her beloved grandfather, Qusamequin. She had always known him as Grandfather Yellow Feather until the Pilgrims changed his name to Massasoit. Her grandfather had gone to live with the great *Kautantowwit* many years back. Perhaps, in some way, the kindly southwest winds had borne this message, a yellow feather, that, like her ancient parent, would say, "Do not give up, my daughter." It could be true, as well, that the crescent moon was about to replenish itself with good news for its children.

Suddenly, as Akayna stood staring out at the night, her bedroom door sprang open. She looked back at the sound. A black man filled the door frame. Akayna recognized him as the dark-skinned one she had seen earlier that day at the marketplace. He was so tall, he had to stoop to enter. What did he want with her?

Akayna stood transfixed as she saw him close the door quietly and motion her to silence. Startled almost to immobility, she gasped. His skin, darkened by his combined African and Moroccan heritage, seared to a burnished ruddiness by the sun and open sea, mesmerized her. Never had she seen such coloring. She could see now it was not paint. His dark chest showed glistening from his open-necked white shirt. She noticed the muscles of his thighs strain against the leather breeches he wore. His feet were encased in leather sandals, and around his close-cropped head he wore a leather band decorated with colorful painted designs. A large brass ring encircled his left upper arm. He wore no weapons.

Akayna backed toward the window, but before she could cry out, in one stride the man had reached her and pulled her into his arms. It was as if he had been driven by an unknown force and nothing could stop him. His mouth sought her soft lips as she struggled to pull herself away from this unexpected assault. Khamseen's arms tightened more possessively as she attempted to free her imprisoned mouth. She kicked at him and tried to scream. She attempted to tear her lips away from his. Her twin braids swung wildly about her head as she twisted and turned. Her struggles were to no avail, because he was strong and determined.

"I'm sorry, I couldn't resist. You are so lovely," he said, when he finally released her.

Akayna was grateful for the brief moment to compose herself. After all, she remembered she was the daughter of a chief, a sachem of the Algonquin tribe. She stood as tall as she could.

"Who are you? I am Akayna, daughter of Chief Anesquam."

"I am Khamseen, a boat builder. I have come to take you home." Home! The word rekindled the ember of hope Akayna had felt when she saw the yellow feather drift into her room.

"Quickly," Khamseen whispered. "Everyone is asleep. Come."

Akayna did not know she was being kidnapped.

CHAPTER SEVEN

The next morning, a confused Akayna realized that once again her life was moving out of her hands and into the hands of someone she did not know. This African, this Khamseen, who was he? Could he really return her to her home? It was all so strange; the extreme heat of this land, the sparkling blue of the Mediterranean, the strange speech of those around her — sailors, merchants, fishwives — bombarded her ears with their patois as she tried to understand them.

She had to remember that she was a sachem's daughter, an Algonquin "child of the first light." Her father, indeed all her kinsmen, were called this because they were Easterners, the first people to see the morning sun. Thus privileged by the god-sun, high expectations were set for the tribe. The code of the ancient fathers was: *Be strong as the light source that shines on us. Be able to do all the good one can do in one's lifetime. Be as wise, as sensible and as knowing as our glorious day-star.*

Akayna vowed to live up to the tribe's teaching. As a sachem's daughter, a subscribed pattern had been set for her. She would marry and someday be Squaw Sachem. She was an only child.

In the bright light of the morning sun, she stood on the *Sea Treasure's* deck and tried to understand some of the astonishing activity around her. This ship, she noticed, was not at all like the clumsy, bedraggled vessel she had been imprisoned on entering Spain. This immaculate ship seemed light, eager to loose its lines and be off on its maiden voyage. The mainsail, sparkling white cloth, snapped in the morning sun; the shorter sail on the mizzen mast was still furled close to the clean wooden mast; the smaller jibs, too, were bound until needed.

Khamseen, the African, was everywhere, directing his crewmen in tightening the shrouds, the lines that stretched from the masthead to the vessel's sides to support the mast.

Akayna noticed the sheen of perspiration on his broad shoulders as he heaved and tugged on the ship's fittings. He worked closely with the men, and Akayna could not help but notice the respect they gave him.

Strange feelings tugged deep inside her as she recalled her feelings when he had kissed her. Was he planning to violate her because he had "rescued" her? She was confused and concerned. If he tried, he'd have trouble.

Warm in a pair of heavy leggings and shawl that Khamseen had provided for her — "We'll get proper clothing for you later," he had said —Akayna leaned closer to the rail of the ship. She looked out at the clear, blue-green water and at the soft blue sky filled with puffy clouds. It all seemed so peaceful, but where was she headed? What lay ahead?

From behind her left shoulder she heard a man's voice.

"If the wind begins to get rough, you might be safer below deck."

She turned to face Khamseen; his face shone from his exertion.

He felt that this Indian girl would bring him luck. He noted with satisfaction that she seemed to be adjusting to everything quite well. Her cheeks were bright with color from the warm sun and her eyes were alert with the innocence of hope. All was bound to go well with this venture.

"It will take long to get to my home?" she questioned.

"I am not certain, my lady." He wiped his face with his bandanna, and Akayna thought she saw a brief frown crease his broad forehead.

"I hope to reach Gibraltar before nightfall." He shaded his eyes with his hands as he looked at the horizon. He spoke again, almost as if to himself. "Must avoid the emir's men, but must take on provisions for at least six weeks."

Akayna's ears perked up when she heard "six weeks." She had hoped for a shorter journey home.

"Six weeks!" she repeated. "It did not take so long to come to this place."

"We must have more than enough food and water in case it should take that long," he answered. "One must always be prepared for the worst, but expect the best!" he added.

His answers only increased her anxiety. "You have made this trip before?"

"Only in my mind, my lady. Many, many years ago, one of my ancient ancestors made this voyage with an explorer of another country, a man named Columbus.

The griots and storytellers of our family have told and retold the legends of that sailing for years. My father, Mustepha, and I shared the vision of someday making such a voyage. Now, I am determined to do it."

"How do you know how to travel in these vast waters?"

She waved her hand toward the open sea. "The sea is so wide, and the boat is so small."

Khamseen hoped that the twinges of guilt he felt for having purloined the emir's ship did not show on his face. He knew, however, he would have done anything he had to do to sail this ship that he had built and loved on her maiden voyage. He had left word at the emir's palace that he had taken the *Sea Treasure* on a trial run. But, if the voyage proved successful, the borrowed craft would be returned and both he and the emir would be wealthier because of the valuable commodities he would bring from the new world. He could not allow such an opportunity to slip by. He would return with the beautiful Indian girl as well. Perhaps the sight of her loveliness would soften the emir's heart.

"To answer your question, I learned navigation from my father. We use dead reckoning, by our compass and by the stars at night. I am confident," he added, "if I follow my father's rules, we will be successful."

"And your father's rules?"

"Well, my father, Mustepha, says, 'a true sailor knows his ship, watches the water, watches the sky and considers the wind.'"

He studied the girl's face to see if she believed him. It was bad enough that he himself was worried, but he did not want anyone else to doubt his ability to reach the new world. Others before him had made the voyage and he was confident he could, too.

He continued his explanation in a firm voice. "I plan to use the trade winds from the east, just like the explorers before us did, to get us to the new world, America."

"How do you find these... trade winds?" The wide open ocean was not at all like her forest home, and she felt bewildered by its vastness.

Khamseen smiled. His white teeth flashed against his dark smooth skin. Even the girl's questions did not bother him. "After we leave the Madeiras," he said, "we will sail true south until it gets hot, or as the explorers say, 'till the butter melts,' and then we change course to the right."

"And you say six weeks?"

"Miss Akayna, if our luck holds and the winds are favorable, we will be in the new world in three to four weeks' time, and you should be at your father's side shortly after that."

Akayna nodded. "I will pray to our Great Spirit that he will help you find the winds you need to do this thing."

• • •

Their luck did not hold. A few days later, Akayna was on deck when she overheard one of the sailors complaining about a woman's presence on the ship.

"'Tis an evil ship we've signed on, mark my word," he said to another seaman as they coiled up the lengths of rope that lay on the deck. "You know," he continued, and nodded in Akayna's direction, "that one could be of the devil himself with her red skin and that long black witch's hair."

"The devil you say?" the other sailor spat into the

ocean and raised his eyes to the sky. "Heaven protect us."

The first sailor continued, more bold and louder than before, aware that Akayna was within hearing distance. "If the master of this ship had to bring a woman aboard, why not an African woman, one of his own kind? An ebony damsel, and more than that, one woman for each one of us, eh?"

A chill of horror raced over Akayna as she listened. How could she be safe among men who saw her as evil? Would they try to kill her, get rid of her? She decided she had better go below, and as she tried to move past the men surreptitiously without bringing more notice to herself, she heard Ibraha, the first mate, reprimand the men. He must have heard their complaints. She stood still, rooted in fear. She could hardly breathe.

"Be quiet, you two!" He suddenly shot out his burly arms with bulging muscles, grabbed each man by the shirt front and lifted each off his feet to face him.

He turned to reassure the young woman Khamseen had told him would be on board the ship. Just like Khamseen! Stealing a boat was not enough. He had to add kidnapping, and a woman at that, to his list of adventures.

My God in heaven, it's her! He recognized the young woman he had seen on the *Morning Star* a few weeks back. *Even in those old leggings and tattered shawl, she is the most beautiful creature I have ever seen.*

Ibraha saw the terror in her face. She did not speak. As he stared at her, he could smell his own sweat as emotional heat rose from his body. Deep in his heart he knew two things. One, the communication that passed between them at that moment was like a flashing bolt of lightning that arched its fiery connection from one to the other as they stood there. It changed them both. Ibraha knew that somehow this woman would be in his future. But, also, Khamseen had seen her first. Ibraha knew that Khamseen's first and overriding ambition was to obtain personal wealth and glory. The woman, well, knowing that Khamseen always thought of himself first, most likely she provided a further challenge to outwit the Englishman to steal her from his house, much as it did to steal the emir's ship! But what if Khamseen *did* want her? Somehow Ibraha knew an impasse in the "older brother" relationship he had with Khamseen would come to an end. His thoughts went back to the set of circumstances that had thrown the two of them together.

• • •

Ibraha had seen it first. A large, dark-skinned, torpedo-shaped body that moved sleekly in the water. He knew immediately that it was a drift whale that had wandered into the shallow waters off the Bay of Biscay.

The whale, feeding on a school of fish moving swiftly ahead of it, had moved too close to shallow waters. Suddenly, it was trapped.

Ibraha shouted, "Whale on starboard side!" and the boat steerer of the small boat wheeled to maneuver the craft, pushing the large animal closer to the shore.

Ibraha and Mustepha, Khamseen's father, watched as the appointed marksman threw his axe to the back of the whale's blowhole. The whale was about fifty feet long, and certainly weighed several hundred tons. There was no escape for the wounded animal that needed deep water to sound in, and it was slowly being crushed by the weight of its own body. White, foaming, bloody streaks of water circled the boat as the whale, in its death throes, tried to dive to safety.

Two of the seamen threw single-barb harpoons at the animal; one pierced a lung and the whale began to drown.

Ibraha had intended to shorten the whale's agony by using a short spear, but it was then that Mustepha stopped him with a flashing knife.

"It's my turn to strike the 'telling blow'!" he shouted as he pinned Ibraha's fingers to the rail with his knife. Ibraha realized then what an explosive temper the man had. He had seen the same quick temper in Khamseen many times when the younger man had felt thwarted.

From a stormy beginning they had reached a satisfying relationship for both, and Ibraha learned to view Khamseen almost as his younger brother.

• • •

Ibraha shook his head to free himself of his memories and muttered a brief prayer for peace, a successful voyage and return. Soon the wind billowed from the northeast and the sails filled as the trim vessel slipped over the rolling waves. They were moving well, Ibraha thought. What would he do with his feelings about Akayna? About Khamseen?

In her cabin, Akayna felt the ship's movement, heard the creaks and groans as the wooden ship danced to meet her future. Akayna wondered again about her own future. Where would she be many moons from now? She prayed to *Kautantowwit*, the Wampanoag god who sent the best winds.

CHAPTER EIGHT

After witnessing the hostile action of the two crew-men, Akayna decided to keep to herself as much as possible. She stayed below during the day and would go up on deck only in the evening, and then in the company of Ibraha or Khamseen.

Before long the ship reached Funchal, the main harbor in the Madeiras. Khamseen had said they would stock up on provisions and recheck the ship before moving from the island, the last port before crossing the ocean. He also indicated if all was clear, no sign of the emir's men, they might remain in the harbor for two days.

"Is there any article you want or need?" he asked Akayna. He seemed concerned about her lack of proper clothing.

"Some sewing cloth, needles and thread," she indicated, making sewing gestures with her hands.

"Would you perhaps like to go ashore?"

"Could I?"

Before this voyage was over, he hoped she would be so grateful to him, she would fall into his arms. *Patience*, he thought; so far she had shown no signs of any feelings toward him. At times he figured she viewed him as little more than a servant. She told him once he would be well paid for returning her to her home.

Khamseen did not know about the privileged status Akayna was accorded by the tribe. Her family's wealth had increased when her mother, Monticut, had married her father, Anesquam. Her mother's land holdings had extended from the shores of Nantucket Sound to the Narragansett Bay and the Providence Plantations.

On the morning of their second day in port, Khamseen suggested that she prepare to take the dory ashore with Ibraha.

Khamseen had told her, "I'm going to send Ibraha with you. He will take care of you and keep you safe. He will be obtaining provisions and supplies that we need, as well as an extra rudder. You may spend the day ashore, if you wish. We'll be leaving this port after dark, before the winds change, because of the day's heat."

With the Portuguese centavos and escudos Khamseen had loaned her, Akayna planned to purchase what she needed. "My father will repay you; I am keeping an accounting," she told him. "It is not the Algonquin way to owe anyone."

Khamseen watched as she walked toward the dory, and Ibraha helped her aboard. Ibraha had been successful in keeping his true feelings for Akayna hidden and under control. He wondered if he would be able to spend a day alone with her without revealing his feelings. It would take all the stamina he had, but now was not the time. Like Khamseen, he wanted to see her returned to her home first.

The short trip was made in silence. He was glad when they finally reached shore. The nearness of

Akayna made him tense.

Akayna was delighted to be on solid ground again. The sea was still strange to her, but she had learned to tolerate it; she had to, since it was her only way home. But to feel the soil beneath her feet, see the trees sway gently in the soft winds, see and hear brightly colored birds singing their songs, brought joy to her heart. She was glad to have this precious little time with Mother Earth. But trouble waited on the shores of Funchal for Akayna.

She noticed that some of the peasants stared at her skin coloring and long black braids, but most smiled pleasantly as she went in and out of the shops, accompanied by the big African, Ibraha. He purchased meat that had been salted in large kegs, fruits, vegetables, dried grains, and casks of water and wine. Their next stop was at a shipfitter's, where Ibraha selected and paid for a new rudder. He carried it to the horse and cart that he had hired. Then he turned and smiled pleasantly at Akayna. "Now, Miss, for your supplies."

In a nearby dressmaker's stall, Akayna found some muslins and heavy cottons, as well as a piece of light wool for a shawl. Using sign language and a few Portuguese phrases that Ibraha knew, the merchant was able to assist her.

Packages in hand, they had started out of the shop when suddenly Akayna came to an abrupt halt. She gasped and grabbed Ibraha's arm so tightly he felt her nails dig into his flesh.

"What is it, Miss?"

Akayna could only breathe in a coarse whisper, "There! Look there!"

"Where? What is it?" He was puzzled by the anxious

hoarseness in the girl's voice.

He followed her shaking finger to where she pointed. He saw two white men seated at a table in an outdoor cafe. They seemed an unlikely pair. One looked rough, unshaven and coarse. He was dressed in soiled clothing and his hair was lank and dirty. The other man was much younger, immaculately dressed and well-groomed. "Who are they, and why are you so afraid?"

"I'm not afraid, Ibraha, I'm angry! That one is Henry Kendall," she pointed out the older man. "He took my father's money to see me safely to my cousin, Rebecca, in England, and that one," she indicated Sir Aidan Stuart, "he bought me from Henry Kendall to be his consort; chatelaine, he called it."

"And it was from his villa that Khamseen rescued you?" Ibraha wanted to know.

Akayna nodded, never taking her eyes from the pair.

"Think they may be searching for you?"

"Yes, yes, I do!"

"Well, quick, hide before they see you!" He looked around the dusty streets filled with vendors and shoppers and sought a spot of refuge for her.

Akayna shook her head. "I will not hide. Algonquins do not hide. 'Face your enemy' my father always said, and that is what I will do."

Ibraha knew the two men were not a threat to him; he'd faced tougher foes. But he couldn't let anything happen to the woman he knew he loved.

"Watch them," she hissed to Ibraha as she stepped into the shadow of the shop. When she returned a few moments later, he was taken aback by her appearance. Her hair was in disarray, a wild cloud all over her head, she had twigs and bits of grass in it. Muddy dirt smeared her face and clothing. Her bare feet and legs bore streaks of mud and debris from the street. She looked terrible, like an abandoned street waif.

"Agree with what I say, Ibraha."

They walked in the direction of the two men. No one on the street could ignore the odd pair. The tall, dark African and the small, bedraggled young women.

They caught the attention of Henry Kendall at once. He had just looked up from his glass of wine and gulped when he recognized Akayna.

"Wal, now, wot 'ave we 'ere?"

He grabbed Sir Aidan's sleeve to call his attention to the pair. "Sir, 'tis the Indian girl from yer villa! Dunno who the bloke is wi' 'er."

Sir Aidan rose from his seat. He could hardly believe his eyes. The girl looked terrible, as if she'd been abused. "Henry Kendall suggested that I might get word of you here," he began. "We were informed that the *Sea Treasure* sailed about a week ago, and we knew this port was a supply depot." He hesitated a bit, then plunged into the matter. "I've come to return you to my villa."

"Never, never!" Akayna started, when Henry Kendall interrupted.

"Ye are 'is propitty, ye know."

Akayna looked directly at the man and spoke firmly. "I belong to this man's captain, Khamseen."

"Ah, he's the one stole ye from the villa, eh?"

"Stolen? No, not stolen. I went with him of my own will because he promised to return me to my father's *wetu*."

"No matter," the surley Kendall spat. "'Tis Sir Aidan 'ere that bought 'n' paid fer ye."

Akayna's face flushed with anger. "I was not for sale! You know my father, Chief Sachem Anesquam, gave you money to take me to London to my kins-woman, Matowaka. She is called Lady Rebecca by the English there. She would have cared for me until my father sent for me. You know that is the truth." She glared at Kendall, her chest rising and falling as her anger peaked. "And you swore on the white man's Bible book!"

Henry Kendall looked at Sir Aidan, who appeared perplexed by what he had heard. His head swiveled from one to the other as he listened. He was also acutely aware of the African, Ibraha, who seemed very con-cerned over the girl. He was large enough, with his muscular build, even with no weapon, to intimidate anyone. And Aidan Stuart had no weapon, and was not likely to use one if he had.

Akayna spoke again in a low quiet voice. The men had to strain to hear her. "I have slept in the African captain's bed." *Great Spirit, forgive my lies,* she thought.

"So," Kendall smirked, "'e's 'ad ye, eh?"

Akayna lowered her head.

Ibraha sensed what Akayna was suggesting to the two duplicitous men. Quickly, he seized the moment. He threw a few escudos on the table between the two, and unceremoniously yanked Akayna away. His voice was gruff. "Come away, girl, back to the ship."

Leaving two open-mouthed Englishmen behind, he pushed Akayna into the cart and hurried to the dory dockside as quickly as possible.

Ibraha chuckled as they stowed their purchases in the bottom of the dory. He picked up the oars, settled them expertly in the water, and as he pulled at them, he remarked to Akayna, "I must tell you, Miss, you were a brave one to face those two."

"Ibraha, I had to do it. It is not the Algonquin way to turn from trouble. The Algonquin faces whatever comes."

"But why did you tell them that you belonged to Khamseen — that you had slept in his bed? You know that is not true." Even as he said the words, Ibraha was unsure. What if she had? Immediately, he was upset by his thought.

"Aha, Ibraha, I fooled you, too!" Akayna's face broke into a mischievous grin. "I knew they would not want me if they thought I had been 'spoiled', especially by a black man. That is why I made myself look so untidy and unclean. I wanted them to think I had been used and abused. But all the while I was praying deep in my heart that the Great Spirit would see the truth there, even though my tongue was forked as I spoke to my enemies."

"You are a clever girl, I think," Ibraha said as he continued to row the dory toward the anchored *Sea Treasure*.

"I could see, Ibraha, that neither of them were men of strength. We Indians can tell by little things — a small nervous movement here, a shift of the eyes there, the timbre of the voice. I knew they were not true men, only shadows of men."

"And your judgment was right. Not only are you brave, but you are clever."

Under his breath he mumbled, "'And I love you for it." His heart ached to speak what was in his mind.

CHAPTER NINE

Ten days later, and three hundred miles off the West African coast, the *Sea Treasure* left the Cape Verde islands and moved blithely into the mid-Atlantic. It made good speed with its sail full and close to the winds.

Khamseen kept the correct bearing, and gave orders to his men accordingly. Most often, either he or Ibraha maintained the helm position, and because they were compatible and understood each other so well, little spoken communication was needed between them. Ibraha was a skilled navigator.

Akayna envied their relationship. It was not that they intentionally excluded her, but they shared a history, a love of ships and the sea that she knew little about.

She missed even more acutely the relationship she had shared with her father. She missed his radiant warm smile, the firm grip of his hand when he helped her over fallen logs as they trudged through their beloved forest. There was comfort in his silences, too, when he told her a story or legend of a long ago happening and waited quietly until she asked for the ending. After her mother's death they had grown closer than before. She wondered if the murderer of Ella Gardner had been found. Had her father sent a message on a sailing vessel to England to tell her to return home?

Ibraha was aware of how the enforced solitude and the feeling of exclusion affected the Indian girl. So he started to talk with her about the navigation of the ship.

He would describe the parts of the vessel and the functions of each part. He was delighted and amazed at how quickly she grasped the mechanics of sailing. He was happy to share time with her, as innocent as it was.

"You see, Akayna, a boat cannot sail straight into the wind. The wind comes from one side or the other. When the wind is from the starboard, or right side of the boat, we call it a starboard tack. The port tack, or left side, is when the wind comes from that side."

"How do you make the ship move in the right direction?" Akayna wanted to know.

"The wheel is connected to the tiller, which helps to steer in the right direction, you see," Ibraha told her, "but our moving power is the wind that propels us. Without a proper wind, we would not be able to sail.

"I am going to remember what you have told me, Ibraha. We have in my family tribe, a storytelling time called *hawkswawney*, usually in the fall. It will likely be that time when we get back. I will be the best storyteller of all," she said proudly.

Ibraha understood her sense of pride. He felt he, too, was learning from her. As he listened to her talk of the green forests and mountains, the sea near her Massachusetts home, he felt close to her, and prayed that all would go well. A twinge of guilt about Khamseen's ultimate intentions nagged at him.

Silently they watched the ship slip over the bosom

of deep-blue water, raising and lowering as it rode the waves.

Ibraha continued his navigational lesson. "Any vessel over ten meters or more will almost always average nearly a hundred nautical miles a day. That is, if the weather is good and one uses the largest sail to catch the wind."

"So, you are saying..."

"I reckon on thirty days to reach your country."

"But, Ibraha, I heard Khamseen talk with you and he seems to have plotted a voyage to the West Indies. My home is not there. Surely he does not intend to trick me?" Her eyes widened at the thought.

"You should ask him," Ibraha said quietly.

She did, a few days later.

"On my word, I intend to take you to Massachusetts. 'The big hill', you call it," Khamseen explained when she questioned him.

"So why are you sailing south?"

"I must tell you the truth, I see, Akayna," he said, and momentarily lost eye contact with her as she questioned him.

"The truth?"

"The truth is the *Sea Treasure* is not my ship."

"Not your ship? I don't understand."

Khamseen took a deep breath. Would she see him as a criminal or as an opportunist. He hoped for the latter. "My father lives the life of a simple fisherman," he began, watching her face for understanding. "For myself, I have always loved the sea, but I have wanted more from it. So I apprenticed myself to a shipbuilder. The *Sea Treasure* is my very first ship."

"But you don't own it."

"No, I do not. It was built on commission from the Emir of Beheri. I have been very worried these past few weeks that perhaps his men would have tracked us to a port, much as Henry Kendall and Sir Aidan did."

"To take the ship back?" Akayna's voice mirrored the tension she felt.

"To take the ship and me back. The punishment for stealing is death, you know."

Akayna's heart dropped like a stone, and she felt cold terror where hope had been. "But the one who owns the ship, this emir..."

"He is not a vindictive man. And in the hold of the *Sea Treasure* I have brass goods, leather, Madeira wine and other goods to sell on consignment for the merchants of the *souk*. I intend to give my share to the emir."

"You think he will accept and forgive you?"

"I hope that he will. I will explain that the *Sea Treasure* is a worthy ship — her sea trial a successful one."

"Why don't you think he will punish you? You took something that belongs to him."

"That is true. But Kendall and Sir Aidan took someone who did not belong to them. You. And I believe when I explain all the circumstances to the emir, he will be merciful toward me."

Akayna realized that the man Khamseen was a risk-taker. She was not certain how much of his dangerous defiance was for her benefit or for his own personal aggrandizement, but she could tell he was a man with selfish goals. Was she one of them? Confused by what she had just learned, she changed the subject. She needed time to sort things out.

"Near my village on the Vineyard Sound are two fine harbors, Popponessett and Waquoit. You should have no trouble entering either. It is not far from there to my father's *wetu*."

Khamseen understood the girl's deep desire to return to her home. He was also wise enough to know if he pressured her by trying to win over her affection, he would most likely fail. It was apparent that for now her home, her father and her tribe were the central realities of her world. Could he, Khamseen, an African, move into that special world of hers? Would she leave all that behind and return to his home with him? What would it take for her to want to do so?

• • •

Binyusef, the Algerian seaman hired by Khamseen as a crew member, had not forgotten his embarrassing rift with Ibraha. To Ushbar, his young cohort, he continued to complain, out of earshot of either Khamseen or Ibraha, about the doomed voyage they were unlikely enough to sign on. To them the two Africans were foreigners and, as Algerians, they should *never* have signed on a ship commanded by Africans. Neither would ever had admitted that each of them had been desperate for a berth on any ship. Now they were committing virtual suicide to be on a ship with a woman aboard.

Binyusef told the impressionable Ushbar, "We will never see Algeria again! Why should we risk our lives on the whim of a man crazy enough to sail with a woman? Her, with the copper skin and hair like a horse's tail!"

The situation worsened when the winds left and they were becalmed. Khamseen ordered the men to lower the useless sails and he assigned tasks for them. He had to keep them occupied.

Empty wine casks were filled with sea water to provide more ballast for the listless ship. The ropes were examined for weak areas and then recoiled. Decks were washed and brass fittings were polished. Every man was busy.

Ibraha's sixth sense told him that something was wrong. He had been around men long enough to recognize a current of distrust. He said nothing to the busy Khamseen, but kept a close surveillance on both Binyusef and Ushbar, especially the older Binyusef. He noticed the Algerian's craftiness, the way he rarely made eye contact when he spoke to anyone.

There was something else, too. He was extremely restless, Ibraha noticed. He slept only in short naps, and when he was on watch he paced erratically. Even his voice was different. There were times when his speech was so rapid, the saliva collected at the corners of his mouth because he didn't take the time to swallow, and he continuously drooled, which made being near him unpleasant. Other times he was almost mute. Ibraha remained alert. Trouble could still follow them.

Ibraha was also acutely aware of Akayna. Ever since the episode at Funchal, he had struggled with his feelings. He knew he loved her and his guilt was compounded by his deep friendship for Khamseen. What would happen if Khamseen should learn of Ibraha's feelings? Khamseen would view it as betrayal, Ibraha knew. If ever he, Ibraha, needed self-control in his life, the time was now. Never, in his wildest dreams, could he have imagined that a tiny slip of a girl from a strange country could affect him the way the Indian girl had.

Because he had watched her closely, he internalized the loneliness, the isolation she seemed to feel. He ached to help her.

On the third day without wind, Ibraha approached Akayna. She had just washed her hair and was drying it as she sat in the sunny warmth near the bow of the boat. Ibraha's heart contracted and beat wildly at the sight. Her long hair hung like a cape of midnight satin around her shoulders as it fell loosely from a center part on her head. As she bent her head back to shake her hair free, Ibraha could see the lovely, sensuous line of her neck, and the simple arching of her body brought into focus the agonizing beauty of her upraised breasts. Ibraha knew she was not aware of him, that her behavior was natural and innocent. He cleared his throat to alert her and spoke quickly.

"Good morning, Akayna. I have something for you."

"A kitten!" she smiled with delight, when he handed it to her. "Ibraha! Where did you get it?" She held out her arms for the soft, wriggling ball of gray and white striped fur.

"He's just being weaned," he told her. "His mother and the rest of his sisters and brothers are in the hold of the ship."

"On the ship?"

"Oh, yes, it's always good to have a mouser on board ship. Like him?"

Ibraha saw the pleasure in her face as she held the kitten close. "I love him. I'm going to call him Panseis; that is Algonquin for warrior. He looks like a brave soldier, don't you think?"

"Indeed. He is the biggest and the strongest of the

litter."

As Akayna stroked and caressed the kitten, Ibraha's emotions almost overcame him as he vicariously experienced the tenderness she showed the animal. How could he ever extinguish the fire he felt in his loins? At that moment the urge to pull her into his hungry arms was so powerful, he could hardly control the desire. He shook his head and moved away quickly, not trusting himself to stay near Akayna any longer.

• • •

Later that same day, Khamseen talked to Ibraha. "I think we are going to have some wind soon." He pointed to the evening horizon. "See that layer of thick clouds? If it thickens and lowers closer to the earth we may have rain, and with it a bit of wind."

"I agree, Khamseen. I should prepare the men."

At that moment Akayna came up the companionway, holding Panseis in her arms.

As the two men stood talking, Ibraha caught a sudden movement in Akayna's direction. Binyusef reached Akayna before anyone knew what was happening and grabbed at the kitten in her arms.

"*Azazel!*" he spat at her. Khamseen recognized the folklore reference to the rebel angel who seduced men. He moved as quickly as he could when he heard Akayna scream, but Ibraha was faster. He lunged toward Binyusef and kicked low on the Algerian's knees. A sharp crack and the pained howl from Binyusef let Ibraha know he had reached his target. Binyusef dropped the kitten and reached for Ibraha's throat. He was strong, but even in his madness he was no match for Khamseen's friend.

Khamseen pushed Akayna back to the safety of the

lower deck and he moved forward to help his friend. He did not see Ushbar creep up behind him with an upraised dagger.

Standing in the well of the companionway, Akayna yelled, "Khamseen, behind you!"

Khamseen turned, shot his arm along the inside of the man's upraised arm, and bent the man's elbow backward until he saw tears of pain in Ushbar's eyes and the knife clattered to the deck. He turned his adversary around, and with a flick of his hand freed his own bandanna from his neck. He used the cloth to tie the man's hands. He grabbed a nearby piece of rope and lashed Ushbar to the rail.

Ushbar struggled as he cried out, "This is a doomed ship with a woman aboard! She-devil! Not even one of our kind!"

A sharp slap from Khamseen stopped the flow of words from Ushbar's mouth, as his head swiveled from the blow. There was no mistaking the anger in Khamseen's eyes.

Ibraha had tied Binyusef, and he lay sprawled on the deck. Binyusef babbled incoherently, unintelligible sounds that made no sense.

The rest of the crew came from other parts of the ship and Khamseen shouted, "Lower the dinghy! Quickly!"

Ushbar suddenly realized his fate and started to beg for forgiveness.

"I will not kill you," Khamseen told the two men when they were put aboard the boat. "Let the fates decide your future." He ordered a cask of water, some loaves of bread and a pair of oars to be put into the boat. As the small boat containing the men was lowered, Khamseen turned to the rest of the crew. "Be warned.

I demand loyalty. Nothing else will do."

The wind came as predicted, sails were raised and the *Sea Treasure* moved forward briskly. A small speck on the horizon was all that could be seen of Binyusef and Ushbar. No one spoke of them again.

CHAPTER TEN

The wind held steady from the northeast. Either Ibraha or Khamseen took frequent readings during the day with the sextant and compass. The sea seemed empty of activity, except for an occasional sea-flying bird. The warm, clear-blue waters were easy to sail upon, and the *Sea Treasure* appeared to be enjoying herself as she made her way.

Sometimes at night, Khamseen pointed out the constellations to Akayna. There were times in those moments when she felt both attracted to and repelled by the man. She wanted to trust him, to believe in him, but there was a hard edge to him that got in the way. She frequently believed he was pleasant to her for a purpose she did not understand.

But Ibraha understood. He knew Khamseen's mind was on the voyage and his chance to escape the clutches of the emir. He knew Khamseen wanted to reach his financial goal and return home with wealth and honor. Khamseen so far had shown only kindly interest in the girl. Ibraha wondered about his true feelings. Would they surface? And when? And what would be his own reaction?

• • •

Later, Ibraha reminded Khamseen that they were indeed nearing land. More birds were being seen, and it was well known that such birds never flew too far from the shore. "I think we should drop anchor soon and send out a boat to find a safe harbor. I have heard of large-sized rocks on the western shore of this island, Barbados," he told Khamseen. "Many ships have been wrecked in those waters."

"Well, then," Khamseen suggested, "you take Zaid with you and make sure of a safe harbor. But we should wait until daybreak. We will anchor then, and you will have more daylight hours for your survey."

The next morning the sun was barely pink streaks of color in the rosy gray sky when Ibraha and Zaid, his young helper. were lowered. Akayna watched as Ibraha, his huge muscles bulging, took up the oars to row. Zaid was at the tiller.

"Good luck!" Khamseen shouted to the small figures in the boat. Ibraha waved his hand in acknowledgment.

Akayna watched until she could see them no longer. She was sorry to lose sight of her friend, Ibraha. She breathed a silent prayer to *Manitou*, God of the sea, to return the men safely. For now, they must wait.

The sun moved higher in the sky, and as the day progressed, Khamseen assigned chores to the remaining crewmen. There was much to be done. Cleaning, polishing, recoiling ropes, tending to the sails and checking the lines. One of the men climbed to the top of the mast. He reported that with the spyglass, Ibraha and Zaid were still in sight.

Akayna spent the day working on her clothing, sewing and mending. She played with Panseis, who would come to her when she called him. He loved to play with her long braids and would bat them back and forth with his paw, especially when she rested on her berth. The dangling braids intrigued the kitten.

Afternoon moved into evening and there was no sign of the men returning. Khamseen, as usual, took the first watch. Akayna, herself, was too excited to remain on deck, so she went below. She was not sure how to do it, but she wanted to ask the gods for their assistance. Deep in her heart she had a feeling of apprehension. Would she ever really get home? It had be so long since she had seen her father's face. He must be concerned. She knew he had not heard from Henry Kendall. He never would. She was certain of that.

She prayed first to *Git-che-man-itu*, the master of life, and to the god of the good wind.

• • •

The following morning, the lookout saw a small boat sailing toward them. Khamseen recognized Ibraha and Zaid, along with a stranger.

"We have a pilot to lead us into the harbor!" Ibraha shouted, as the boat came within hearing distance.

Akayna saw Ibraha and felt her heart pound with relief. She realized how much she had missed him.

Khamseen acknowledged the information with a wave and instructed his crew to "up anchor." The sails were trimmed and the *Sea Treasure* skipped behind the pilot boat.

Akayna noticed the large rocks, some as large as a long house, on the Atlantic coast of the island. Now she could see why caution had been taken. There was no safe harbor there, only heavy swells and a churning surf that would threaten any ship.

Soon they rounded the island into the soft blue waters of the Caribbean. Akayna had never seen a land so lovely. The soft, warm Caribbean air engulfed and soothed her. She was enchanted by the delicately-green causerina trees that swayed gently in the breeze from the distant hills. Heavy blossoms colored orange, yellow, pink and purple from bougainvillea, flamboyant and hibiscus trees, paraded like ladies in their Sunday finery on each side of the street.

Surely, Akayna thought, *Kautantowwit,* god of the best winds, must have touched this place. She felt a strange peace. As they neared the dock, she could see the busy marketplace with brown-skinned people milling about. The activity amazed her. Never had she seen so many human beings!

When she arrived at her father's *wetu* and the tribe gathered to listen to her accounting, she would have as many stories to tell as there were beads on her father's wampum, his storytelling belt.

CHAPTER ELEVEN

Khamseen faced several problems that made him decide not to linger on the fascinating island of Barbados. His overriding goal to get Akayna home was always on his mind, but added to that was the possibility of being pursued by the emir, or his men, and the recently acquired knowledge that he could be sailing up the Atlantic coast in uncertain weather. He would be lucky if he could get past the treacherous seas of Cape Hatteras off the coast of North Carolina.

An old gnarled "Bajan" seaman told him that the day after the *Sea Treasure's* arrival. The native had been mending some nets. He had taken time from his work to smoke his pipe, and when he noticed Khamseen standing nearby, recognized him as a stranger. He showed a friendly curiosity toward the African as he spoke to him. "And you, stranger, where be your home?"

He nodded knowingly when Khamseen told him Northern Africa. "That be the mother home of most of us here on this island. I be free, me and my family, but many of us snatched from home still be slaves of the English. You stayin' 'ere?"

"Oh, no. I am on my way to America. I plan to leave on the first high tide on the morrow."

"You pick a sorry time."

"How so?"

"You know about hurricanes?"

"I have heard of such winds. They come now?"

"My son," the old seaman drew on his pipe, "you mayhap have had bad winds in Africa, I've no doubt, but the wind and rain of a hurricane will be the worst you'll ever live through."

He puffed thoughtfully on his pipe as he sat on a low stool. There were crushed seashells at his feet, and his large brown toes were dusted through his open-toed sandals from the scattered flakes.

"See, there," he stood and pointed the stem of his pipe toward the cobalt blue ocean. "Calm, she is now, but if the winds blow strong from the Azores, pick up strength from the ocean, and if they should funnel 'round the equator, be on your guard. The worst may be, too, that she'll be with you all the way north, 'less she dies out over the cold Atlantic."

"Have you sailed through such times?" Khamseen asked.

"Aye, since a boy of twelve. My master, an English captain by the name of Sinclair, took me as his cabin boy on many a voyage. By the by," he put out his hand to Khamseen, "my name is Athellstan Sinclair. My friends call me Stan an' my enemies — well," he smiled as the two men exchanged a firm handshake. "But, yes," he continued, "I've sailed to America and did live to tell the tale of comin' through a hurricane. The best you can do is lash down, tie down everything an' everybody, pray to your favorite god an' ride it out."

Khamseen recognized the truth of the old sailor's words. It added a heavier layer of worry for him. Would luck still be with him? The future was truly a mystery. What was ahead for them?

He thought a good meal onshore might make a decent memory for them. If indeed they did survive. He decided to keep his anxieties to himself. That night he invited Ibraha, Akayna and Zaid to dinner in the capital city of Bridgetown. It was safer for him to have the other two men along; he did not trust himself alone, yet, with Akayna. It was a fearsome struggle with his emotions, but he was determined not to confuse her with the deep feelings he had for her.

Sinclair, the freed sailor, told Khamseen that his older sister, Jessica, also a freed slave, had a small house near the careenage. She often served meals there to sailors, merchants and tradespeople who wanted good food.

A polite but curious crowd gathered around the little group and watched as they entered Mistress Sinclair's home. All eyes were on Akayna. She was striking in a simple cotton tunic that she had fashioned from a bolt of nankeen. The yellow cotton material hung loosely from her shoulders to mid-calf. The sunny color warmed her exposed skin into tones of apricot and peach, the fruity blushes heightened by the stark blue-blackness of her hair. Khamseen's heart filled with pride as he heard the murmurs of approval from the onlookers.

Mistress Jessica Sinclair, a friendly, full-bosomed matron, welcomed them with an amiable smile and gave them a favored table with a view of the careenage. Several small boats were docked there for repairs. All activity had stopped because of the evening hour.

"Tonight, my lady and gentlemen," she announced to them, "we have fresh pumpkin soup seasoned with a bit of lime juice, we have couscous, just cooked, island fish and peppers, or mayhap you would like curry goat and rice."

She looked at each of them for a response, and getting none, continued her recitation. "Of course, we have chicken, shrimp and our island lobster."

Each one looked at Khamseen. After all, they were his guests. He ordered for them all.

The orange-colored pumpkin soup came to them hot and rich with flavor. The hint of lime juice enhanced it with a piquant taste that added to its goodness.

Khamseen was not sure that Akayna realized what meat she was eating, but after the plain shipboard fare they had endured the past few weeks, she seemed to enjoy the subtle-tasting goat meat and broth. The rice had been cooked with small peas and reminded both Ibraha and Zaid of a similar dish from their native Morocco. Couscous, a side dish made from corn meal, was familiar to them all.

Tears of homesickness welled in Akayna's eyes as she recalled the very last time she had prepared a dish of maize for her father. She bent over her food and tried to blink away the tears so as not to disturb the others. As Khamseen watched her eat, he noticed her hesitancy, as if she were afraid to enjoy the meal. He could see, in spite of his attempts to reassure her, that she was very concerned about her future.

Akayna's eyes drifted around the room at times. It was obvious that the people she saw were strange to her. She noticed the smooth ebony of the skin of some of

them, like Khamseen, Ibraha and Zaid. Then she could
see others that were not so dark, but brown in their skin
color. Like a walnut, some were very lightly tanned and
others had pale, freckled skin. Some even had red or
blond hair.

What kind of people were they, she wondered. What
tribe? All of her tribe looked very much alike; the same
skin coloring and the same straight, black hair. "May I
ask you about these people, Khamseen?" she spoke in
a low voice. "What tribe are they? They do not look
like other human beings I have seen."

Ibraha smiled at her innocence. Perhaps she had not
seen the mixing of races. Before Khamseen could answer, Ibraha spoke. He had sensed her confusion as he
watched her look at the natives. "You know about your
own family, your Algonquin tribe," he told her, "where
everyone looks the same. But these people are a mixture
of the races."

Akayna shook her head. In her tribe, a "half-caste"
would be ostracized and taunted by others in the tribe.
These people seemed to be comfortable with their differences. She recalled the shame heaped upon a girl
from her clan who had borne a child as a result of a rape
by a settler. The child, a boy, had fair, white skin, and
blue eyes, but had its mother's black Indian hair. Only
four days old, the elders of the tribe decided it would
be better not to keep such an "imperfect" child alive.
If it lived, it would be ostracized and taunted by others
in the tribe. So it had been placed in a little spruce-bark
canoe, moss stuffed into its mouth so that its feeble cries
could not be heard. Akayna could still hear the haunting
cries of its mother as she mourned the child taken from
her. The bereft young woman could do nothing, because

if she had attempted to keep the child, she would have been sentenced to death. The tribe would not support an undesirable child.

Ibraha continued, "These people are rooted in the African race, but through slavery and other means they have become all colors and shades."

As they left the Sinclair house, some young natives were seated on the pilings around the careenage, playing various musical instruments. The concertina's sound was not familiar to Akayna, but the drums spoke to her heart. She was learning much about the world and the people in it.

• • •

Early the next morning the *Sea Treasure* skipped blithely over the ocean, leaving the small, friendly island behind. Akayna knew she would never see any place like it again.

She busied herself playing with Panseis. She started to make some baskets out of the native reeds Zaid had gathered for her in Barbados. She was content to be going home, at last. Khamseen had promised that they should be there in a few more days.

But the next twelve hours changed that promise. There were some scattered clouds in the sky and about half of the time the sun shone through. However, the increasing winds were beginning to worry Ibraha, who was at the helm. He could also see the thick towering clouds forming in the distance, extending to lofty heights.

He sent one of the men below to wake Khamseen. A sleepy Khamseen came up to the helm, but became quickly alert when he followed Ibraha's pointing finger.

"The winds have started to move westward, working

away from the equator, I think," he told Khamseen. "If they change to the north, they may push us to the right and off our forward direction."

"Hold steady as you can, Ibraha," Khamseen told him. "I must warn the men to latch down everything; first we must reef the sails. All hands on deck!" he shouted. "Lower and reef the sails so they will draw some wind, but be prepared to furl them quickly if I give word."

All the men hurried to their tasks, aware that a storm was on the way. Who would know when they would have fair winds and fair skies again?

It had started to rain. The heavy cloud cover was almost directly overhead. The slippery deck threatened their stability as their hands feverishly tied down with heavy ropes anything that might move.

Khamseen hurried below to Akayna. "You must get on your berth, little one. A bad storm is coming and I must tie you to your berth!"

"Tie me? Whatever are you saying, Khamseen?"

"A storm such as none of us have ever seen is upon us, I fear. We must all be tied down, even Ibraha must be tied to the wheel or he could be thrown overboard."

Akayna saw the concern in Khamseen's face. He helped her to settle on the berth and wrapped a heavy blanket over her, pulled two wide straps from beneath the berth, secured one over her arms and upper body, and the other over her thighs. His hands trembled as he touched her body. He could hear the *Sea Treasure* begin to cry with creaks and shudders of her wooden beams as she rode the furious waves. Would his beloved ship meet her greatest test? He tore himself away from Akayna's wide dark eyes with a groan of despair. Had it all been a foolish undertaking? Were they all doomed because of his ambition?

As he ran up the wet companionway, his boots echoed the fearful throbs of Akayna's heart. She prayed to the great god, *Manitou.* It was all any of the small crew of the small wooden ship could do — pray to whatever god would listen.

• • •

Heavy slashes of gray-green sea water flooded the decks of the *Sea Treasure.* Khamseen had directed that all sails be reefed and furled, that all lines and riggings be secured. As the cold waves became higher and the troughs deepened, it seemed the ship would surely touch the ocean floor. Then she would raise her bow sprit as if in a challenge to the warring seas, wind and dark sky. The gallant little ship tried to stay the course.

Ibraha had tied his feet with heavy ropes to the wheelpost, and as the wheel turned in the fury of the storm, he would loosen his hands from it and try to grab the wheel again as it came to center rest. His strong upper arms and shoulder muscles demanded relief from the strain, but he could not give way. He could scarcely see through the wall of driving rain. He could feel the ship's rudder as it hung helplessly and wavered when the stern was free of the water, and he could sense the thrusting bite as the rudder tried to purchase some hold of the water. Ibraha's face burned from the slashing wind, and its roaring sounds seemed like a thousand drums in his ears.

From the corner of his eye, he could see Khamseen trying to crawl toward him. The man would disappear for a moment as the ship rode high and would hang over a forty-foot crested wave. Then Khamseen's body slid forward as the ship plunged down into a seemingly endless abyss. Back and forth, as the ship struggled, it seemed Khamseen's only hope was in getting near enough for Ibraha to make a frantic reach for him. After several futile attempts, Khamseen came close enough for Ibraha to grasp him.

The two men struggled to maintain a hold on the elusive wheel as it threatened to rip their arms from their shoulder sockets. Each time the *Sea Treasure* dipped into the steep sea with the uncertain crests, the men would try to turn the wheel so as to meet the wave.

"We'll be driven... hard into the water... if we don't keep the wheel turned!" shouted Ibraha.

Both men were drenched and their wet hands slipped around the wooden wheel.

"Can we... set an angle... make a crosspath... over the waves?" Khamseen gasped. "Heavy seas... rushing us..."

"Stern comes up high... rudder... no grip!" Ibraha shouted over the howling winds.

Ibraha screamed into Khamseen's ear, "Need a drogue... sea anchor... *anything* to slow us down!"

Khamseen nodded and released his grip on the wheel. It tore at Ibraha's arms as he did so. Khamseen slid rapidly on all fours toward the stern as the boat rose again in the water. He tossed a sea anchor that the men had made out of old pieces of tightly wrapped wood and tied with a thick rug. They had no idea when they had fashioned it during a quiet time at sea that they would so desperately need it. Khamseen hoped that it would be enough to check the *Sea Treasure* from broaching through the water.

Below deck the frightened crew was still tied into

their bunks. It had been difficult to do, but they had managed to swing the wide straps from beneath their bunks and secure themselves. Terrified of drowning, most of them were silent, breathless almost, as they heard the valiant *Sea Treasure* struggle to maintain herself. Sea water, debris, loose articles of clothing washed around the bottom of their bunks and showered them with a bone-chilling spray as the violent motion continued.

It seemed a lifetime, but a half hour later the storm suddenly curved away from their path. The wind lessened, the rain became less driven. To the men, frozen in fright, it seemed a merciful respite, at last.

The *Sea Treasure* climbed one last wave and settled to a slight roll as she moved into less agitated seas.

Ibraha and Khamseen, their faces broken into wide grins, realized the hurricane had veered off at last. Behind them they could see streaks of light. The worst was over.

Khamseen shouted to the men below, "Make sail!"

Zaid and the others ran up the stairs, blinking the water from their faces, and began to loosen the sails and hoist them by their halyards. It seemed as if the *Sea Treasure* herself was proud of her performance, and she began to sail with the wind. Khamseen continued to give his orders to the men and, satisfied that all was as it should be, rushed to check on Akayna. How had she fared during the violence of the hurricane?

He stepped into water up to his ankles and noticed bits of vomitus in the water. Akayna lay pale and unmoving. Her hair was wet and lank, her clothes soaked despite the heavy blanket. Her eyes were closed.

Khamseen gasped with fear as he slashed the webbed

straps with his knife. "Don't let her be dead!" he prayed. His face contorted with anxiety. He picked up the limp body and rushed up the companionway.

Ibraha saw him coming with the unconscious girl in his arms. He beckoned to Zaid to take the wheel.

"Dead! Ibraha, she's dead!" Khamseen keened.

Ibraha took the girl from Khamseen's arms and brusquely turned Akayna over so that her head hung lower than the rest of her body. He gave two or three brisk blows to her back between her shoulder blades and the girl gasped. She started to cough and vomit in strident spasms. Ibraha wiped the vomitus and mucus from her face and struck her again on her back. As air rushed into her lungs, color returned to her face. She continued to cough. Finally, she blinked her eyes.

With a quick reaction, Khamseen pulled the girl into his arms and held her close. His eyes were filled with tears as he looked at Ibraha. He had not anticipated his own deep reaction, nor was he prepared for the look on Ibraha's face. *He loves her!,* he thought. *Ibraha loves her!*

Inwardly, Ibraha berated himself because he realized he had let his love for Akayna show on his face. He knew Khamseen had recognized the transparent emotion he had felt, as clearly as if he, Ibraha, had spoken aloud. *I was careless,* Ibraha thought, *to let my love for Akayna be so obvious, but how can I hide what is in my heart? Khamseen is like my own brother, but we love the same woman. Oh, fateful day that he sent me to Funchal with her!*

Ibraha rose slowly and walked, wordlessly, toward the companionway. He knew his relationship with Khamseen would never be the same.

• • •

Ibraha and Akayna could hardly avoid one another. The *Sea Treasure* was too small a ship. However, he made every attempt to avoid her. He insisted on taking the watch often so that he would be busy at the wheel whenever Akayna might be on deck. No longer did he try to spend time with her explaining the functions of the ship, their current position in the water or their progress toward her homeland. But he could hear her happy, tinkling laugh as she played with her kitten, Panseis, or chatted with the young boy, Zaid. Many times she busied herself up on the sunny deck with her basket weaving. Ibraha delighted in watching her from his place at the wheel as she sat cross-legged on the foredeck. Her skilled fingers formed baskets of beautiful designs. Frequently she used bits of cloth, ribbons and string, even strands of her own black hair, to decorate her work. Ibraha admired her ability to keep herself occupied.

The ocean had finally relented. The hurricane they had come through had tested the *Sea Treasure* and she had proved worthy. Now it was as if the Atlantic offered a kindly apology to the stalwart ship and her crew. It bore them gently and smoothly in a northeasterly direction on its Gulf Stream current of warm flowing water.

One sunny afternoon Ibraha found Zaid busily mending sails that had been ripped during the storm. He hunkered down beside the boy, who acknowledged the older man's presence with a friendly grin. "You like being with Akayna, eh, lad?" He ruffled the boy's curly hair with his hand.

"Aye, Ibraha, I do. She is like one of my sisters. I'm always glad to be with her. She has a lot of things to tell me about her home." His eyes glistened excitedly as he continued. "Has she told you about her home, about how the leaves of the trees change color from green to bright yellow and gold?"

"Oh, yes, she did tell me about that," Ibraha concurred.

"And did she tell you that sometimes when the heavens turn gray and cold, white flakes fall down from the sky and turn the earth to white? Did she tell you that? What a strange sight that must be!" Zaid was like a small child, bursting to share his new knowledge.

"I had heard that before, Zaid," Ibraha explained. "English sailors in Torremolinos have said that it is called 'snow'. They told how it happens many times during the season that they call 'winter' in America. That's where we are going, you know. But I was also told that when the sun gets strong, the white earth warms again and changes back to green, all new once more. The English say it is even somewhat different from their own country, England. More intense, they say."

"I can't wait to see this new place, Ibraha, see the white earth. Will we see it, do you think?"

Ibraha laughed at the boy's enthusiasm. He'd often thought he'd be happy to have a son like Zaid; bright, energetic, and eager to learn of the world and its ways. "It may well be, son, that you will see these new things. They say the rhythm of the changing seasons lessens the boredom of one's life in that part of the world." He wondered as he spoke the words if he would wish for "boredom" before this whole adventure ended.

It was a few days later that he could not avoid Akayna. She ran up the stairs and he mumbled an apology as he stepped aside. Her beauty made him catch his breath. Her thick black hair tumbled about her face as she ran forward, not seeing him coming down the stairs. Her hours in the sun had burnished her skin so it glowed with a healthy red-brown patina. As he moved quickly from her path, he saw the question, the reproach in her eyes. *'Why aren't you my friend anymore? What have I done to make you put me aside like this?'*

She could not have known the strength Ibraha had to summon from within himself to keep from enveloping her in his arms and tasting the exquisite sweetness of her tender lips. How he wanted her! To be his, and his alone, to be far away from the confines of this now too-small ship that Khamseen had built and stolen. What a fool he had been to cast his lot on such an ill-fated and ill-prepared voyage. He was afraid he would go mad with his yearnings for this beautiful Indian girl. Of all the hardships Ibraha had faced in his lifetime — hunting whales, avoiding pirates and thieves on the high seas, sailing through treacherous winds and high-crested waters — none tore at his soul and body more than this... to control his feelings for this lovely being that had entered his life.

It came to a head a few nights later. Ibraha had been relieved of his watch by one of the other trusted seamen, and he stopped briefly before heading down the companionway to his bunk in one of the forward berths he shared with the crew. It was a night of magnificent splendor. The moon was round, full, and a dazzling white. Its reflection on the ocean's rolling waves offered a silver path that stretched to the far horizon. Ibraha knew from his calculations that they were nearing land. He hoped that his personal nightmare would somehow come to an end.

He drew deep, satisfying breaths of the salty air and listened to the rhythmic groans and creaks of the ship's wooden beams. The ship and the ocean had become one as the vessel seemed to touch the wind, grasp it firmly with her sails, and ride smoothly toward her goal.

Ibraha continued to stand with his back to the stairway as he looked out over the gentle whitewash that trailed in the sparkling, diamond-crested billows from the *Sea Treasure's* stern. It calmed his troubled mind, somewhat.

"Why do you avoid me, Ibraha?" Akayna's voice sounded firm and quiet in Ibraha's ear. It startled him from his reverie.

"Avoid you? Not really, but I have been concerned about you. How are you after that ordeal with the storm? Feeling well?"

"Yes, I'm well, but I have missed you. The talks we used to have... have I done something to offend you?"

The innocence in her voice unsettled Ibraha even more. He shook his head slowly and leaned his hands on the ship's railing behind him, almost unable to keep from crushing Akayna in his arms.

"You could never offend me, Akayna," he offered. "It's not in your nature."

The moonlight glinted on her black hair and brought glorious silver tints to it; her tawny skin glowed softly in the moon's shimmering lights, and Ibraha could see her large trusting eyes asking him, pleading with him, for some understanding.

He could not control himself any longer. Brusquely, he pulled her toward him. He kissed her hungrily, drank deeply of the forbidden sweetness of her curving full lips. He ground her body to his as if to physically bind her in a weld so strong it could not be broken. He heard her gasp, as he released her as suddenly as he had taken her. He groaned hoarsely, "That's why I've left you alone," as he thundered blindly down the stairs.

Neither of them saw the dark scowl on the face of Khamseen as he leaned on the beam of the mainsail. Enveloped in the quiet night, he had seen it all. Would he have to act soon to claim the woman he wanted... that should rightfully be his?

CHAPTER TWELVE

The brilliant, breathtaking blue of the autumn Cape Cod sky astonished Khamseen. Even more dramatic to him were the colors of the trees — the golden maples, fiery oaks and yellow birch. Flanked by the sober green of the scrub pines, it seemed to Khamseen that a glorious curtain had been let down by the heavens.

This was Akayna's home. No wonder she wanted to return to this delightful place. Even the *Sea Treasure* was more vivacious and animated as the crisp air billowed her sails. Unexpectedly, Khamseen felt that he belonged here. Perhaps because he wanted Akayna, he could see merit in what she loved.

As he stood at the ship's wheel, he could see the coastline. A sandy beach that cut away toward the radiant woods in the background. In the distance, he could see small farms with what seemed to be long houses surrounded by smaller, hide-covered, tent-like structures.

The night before, anchored out in the harbor, Ibraha and he had talked about what lay ahead. Ibraha had some concerns about the future. Khamseen had listened intently and realized that his friend had never questioned him about what others may have called a "wild goose chase." He believed, too, that Ibraha thought he had hidden his feelings for Akayna very successfully. Somehow they had reached a crossroad in their relationship.

So both men had stood, their arms resting on the ship's rail, as they looked out at the land they had sought for so long. Zaid and the other crew members were asleep below deck, anxious to go ashore the next day.

Akayna had indicated her wish to go into the harbor at first light. She had already packed her few belongings for disembarkation. She was not aware that she was on the minds of both men.

Suddenly Ibraha turned his back to the shoreline. His voice was quiet and measured as it carried out over the water. The solemnity with which he spoke alerted Khamseen and he, too, turned from the rail to look at his friend. "Have you decided what to do now that we are here, Khamseen?"

"Do about what, Ibraha?" Khamseen was aware of what his friend referred to, but until almost that very moment, he had made a conscious effort not to think of the future. What was to be, would be.

"Do you plan to stay here, in America, the new world? 'Tis a long journey from Torremolinos, you know."

"I know. But there is the matter of returning the emir's rightful property, the *Sea Treasure.*"

"I could do that for you," Ibraha offered. "But what about the girl, Akayna? Have you spoken to her, declared yourself to her? I know your feelings toward her, Khamseen, but does *she* know?"

Khamseen's face flushed with embarrassment at the implication of timidity from Ibraha. "I have hesitated to speak because I knew of her concern to reach her father and her home. Also, Ibraha, we are not of the same people, but I have hoped that if she saw how much I wanted to do in her behalf, she would see how much I cared. I mean, all the risks and troubles I was willing to take for her, perhaps she would put the differences aside."

"But if you don't tell her how will she know? You must speak soon," Ibraha insisted. "When you finally speak, she may wonder why you waited so long."

Khamseen sighed, rubbing his face with both hands. He seemed weary. "I know, Ibraha, but I fear that she might deny me. I could not live with that."

Khamseen's words churned in Ibraha's mind as the phrase echoed in his ears, "*could not live with that.*"

Ibraha had never married, but had had his share of romantic liaisons — none, however, serious enough to make him want to marry and give up the sea. Would that he could, because, to his distress, he had discovered the woman he wanted. He had been aware of his feelings even before the confrontation in Funchal with the scoundrel, Henry Kendall, and the weak Sir Aidan. But the bravado, resourcefulness, wit and courage he had seen Akayna display on that day was not like anything he had encountered in any other woman. He knew he had loved her from the first moment he saw her.

As he thought about her, a clear picture of her love-liness rose in his mind and he recognized the unbridled passion for her stirring in his body. How could it be that he should love and desire the same woman as his friend? What could he, or should he, do about this agonizing dilemma?

"Khamseen," Ibraha broke the silence between them, "speak soon, or it may be too late." *The sooner he speaks, the better for all of us,* he thought.

Khamseen nodded thoughtfully. "Tomorrow I will see that she returns to her father's home. I will speak with him first and then to her. I do not know her people's ways, but they must see she means life to me."

Ibraha shuddered inwardly with a feeling of foreboding. Something told him that the past weeks of rough seas, mutiny, and the attempted kidnapping had been nothing compared to what might lay ahead. "If you want to stay here in the new world, I will return and make a report to the emir. You know you have done well, Khamseen. You have done something few men have even attempted. You have sailed the big sea to the new world. Portuguese, Spanish, English, and Dutch have done it, and now you, an African, have done so. I am proud of you."

Grateful for the compliment, Khamseen placed his hand on Ibraha's arm. Ibraha almost pulled his arm away from Khamseen's touch. His miserable guilt was becoming a wedge between them. He would have to leave this place soon.

"Thanks to good fortune, and to you, my friend," Khamseen continued, unaware of Ibraha's discomfort, "I will have several hundred pounds after I pay the men and you. I shall still have an acceptable sum to send to the prince. And the ship should not return with an empty hold. We should send goods for sale there."

"Shouldn't you keep a substantial amount... to start a business here?"

"I won't need much. This is a new country, and from

what I can see, and what Akayna has said, the forests are deep with trees. Shipbuilding should not be hard to do here. This seems to be a good harbor, too."

"Good luck in whatever you do," Ibraha sighed.

• • •

The next morning several canoes, each filled with six or seven Indians, came out to meet the *Sea Treasure.*

Akayna had been waiting on deck since the first grey-pink light streaks creased the morning horizon. She wore her hair in twin braids and had secured a turquoise and leather band around her forehead. Her hopsacking tunic hung loosely from her shoulders. Against the early morning chill, she wore a rose tinted soft linen shawl that she had purchased in Barbados.

Ibraha's eyes were fixed on Akayna. She was straining eagerly, looking for familiar faces of her tribesmen in the approaching canoes. She was like a winged bird, fluttering to leave the nest. He knew this precious creature would soon be gone from his sight. He dared not go near her.

The men in the canoes immediately recognized their sachem's daughter and welcomed her with upraised oars and whooping yells. They waited until she and Khamseen were seated in the lead canoe before welcoming her.

Akayna spoke to the head oarsman, "I am returned," she said.

Because the Indians always spoke in the first person singular, the head oarsman spoke for them all when he responded, "I rejoice."

• • •

As a Wapanachki, or Wampanoag — the French had changed the Indian sound to a softer cadence —

Akayna's father, Anesquam, was a proud man. He did not flaunt his position as sachem, but let his actions speak for him.

On this "Indian summer" morning, he stood in the opening of his *wetu*. He watched his daughter approach, accompanied by a strange-looking man whose skin was as black as night. He had too much dignity to stare. The deep emotion he felt on seeing his lost daughter gripped him so fiercely, he felt the frantic beating of his heart would choke him. It was futile to try to hold back the tears that welled in his eyes. It was like seeing his beloved wife, Monticut, again.

Tears fell freely from his daughter's eyes, however. Her cheeks glistened from the moisture. The changes she saw in her father alarmed her. This man was a stranger. Still tall, still erect, but there was a frailty to him that she had never seen. His usual ruddy complexion was sallow, almost jaundiced, and his deep brown eyes were hollows of despair. His hair hung limp and lifeless around his face. Instead of being jet black as she remembered it, it was flat, dull and gray. This was her strong, masterful, beloved father — the Chief Sachem of the Wampanoags?

Akayna slowly walked toward her father, as if to someone she did not know. The ranking elders of the tribe watched silently. They stood in double rows on either side of the path to the chief's doorway. Their eyes were on Khamseen, as well as on Akayna. There was a low rumble of mutterings as they saw the tall man with the black skin.

Akayna spoke, "I am here, Father."

She was surprised to hear her father give thanks to the Great Spirit. When had he given up the English

God? Since he had become a "praying" Indian, he had not prayed to *Gi-che-man-itu*, the master of life, the Great Spirit. Something had changed him. She could see the ravages of deep suffering line his face.

She knew she had changed as well. Gone was the innocent, naive forest girl who had been hustled from her home. She stood this day on the threshold of womanhood, aware that in her young years she had seen much, traveled to the other side of the world and back, had glimpsed worlds unknown to her father, and had weathered many crises.

Then she remembered Khamseen. "Father, this is Khamseen. It is because of him that I am home."

She saw the struggle appear on her father's face as he tried to grapple with the sight of the dark-skinned man. This was the first black man he had ever seen. How had he burned his skin to make it that color? Was it war paint?

Khamseen stood erect; he knew he was under scrutiny. He nodded, but remained silent. Then Anesquam raised his right hand, palm facing toward his daughter's rescuer. "*N'Tschu!* My friend!" He turned and led the way into his *wetu* as the group of onlookers parted respectfully.

CHAPTER THIRTEEN

It took Khamseen a few moments to adjust his eyes to the dimly lit room inside the Indian home. It was a long, low-ceilinged room made of rough logs. There was a window-like opening at the far end. A flap of some type of animal skin usually covered it in inclement weather, but now it had been pulled to one side to allow light and air to enter. Along the walls were piles of bear skins and buffalo hides used for sleeping. A hole in the brush roof allowed smoke from the central fire pit to escape.

There was to be a meeting of the tribal elders that evening, but the afternoon would be spent in feasting and rejoicing for the great sachem's daughter's safe return.

Squaws came into the sachem's lodge, bearing huge pots of succotash, a dish of corn and beans, potatoes baked in their skins, and dried pumpkin that had been boiled and sweetened with maple sugar from the sugar maple trees. There were boiled green beans, squashes and cabbages stewed in very little water and covered with large leaves of the pumpkin vine to facilitate the steaming process. Preserves of cranberries, dried apples and raspberries were set out, along with all the other foods, on a deerskin covering placed on the floor.

Smoked fish, roasted venison, turkey and chicken were part of the main meat course. In addition, a game pie of squirrel, rabbit and quail, covered with a corn-meal pastry, had been baked in hot ashes.

Khamseen had never tasted such food. The flavors and mixtures were different to him, with the exception of the gamey taste of venison which reminded him of a native goat dish from Morocco, and the cornmeal dish which resembled couscous, an African dish his mother used to prepare. He had never tasted some of the vege-tables and fruits, such as apples and cranberries. He liked the piquant flavor of the tiny red berries. He was offered a drink made from the sarsaparilla root. It was strange to his palate, but he enjoyed it.

He accepted each dish as it was presented to him on crude wooden plates. There were few utensils, but Khamseen was accustomed to using his fingers. He was aware of the strange looks the servers gave him. He noted, as well, they seemed reluctant to touch his skin. He surmised they were afraid his color would rub off onto them. Even small children, trying to get a glimpse of the black man, took bold peeks into the long house where the elders feasted.

Khamseen looked for Akayna and wondered where she was. As he searched the room, he noticed only men were present. Akayna seemed to have disappeared with some of the women of the tribe. He began to sense that ''men first'' was a custom in this community.

Anesquam spoke. His English was interspersed with words from his native tongue. *''N'mamenthshi*, I re-joice on my child's safe return.''

The African's English had been learned from listening and conversing with the "limey" sailors on the docks of Torremolinos, but he understood the chief, whose English was a little more formal, very well.

The meal took most of the afternoon. Anesquam called for his calumet, a fancy smoking pipe made with a long stem reed with a pipe bowl inserted at the end. It was highly decorated with ribbons, leather thongs and colorful feathers. It reminded Khamseen of his father's *hookah*, and he noted the peaceful satisfaction which the sachem seemed to derive from it.

After sending wreaths of smoke skyward for thanks to the Great Spirit, Anesquam turned again to his guest. His eyes squinted and became hard when he heard of Henry Kendall's treachery.

"*Att 'ane, l'ewi*, it cannot be true that the *gesptschat*, fool, Kendall believed he could deceive me."

"I think," Khamseen replied, "he did not believe he would be found out. It was for money that he tried to sell your daughter."

"*Kehella*, aye, yes, now I mistrust all the English. They are encroaching on our lands, steal from our fields that our squaws have planted and tended." He spat on the ground in anger. "*Pah*, they even want to tell us when and how to fish and hunt! And they say the laws they brought with them say it must be this way. You have these English in your land?"

"Yes, there are many, but there are more of us with the skin blackened by the sun. See," Khamseen rubbed his forefinger along his arm, "it does not come off. This is the color I came into the world with. I do not burn in the sun as easily as the whites."

"He is here, you know," Anesquam said.

"Here? Who? Henry Kendall?"

"The same. I have not seen him. I do not wish to spoil my eyesight by looking on such a putrid animal. I believed him when he swore on the holy word of his God that he could be trusted. There is no greater evil than to have words of lies and deceit fall from one's mouth. I will not let his shadow stand between me and the sun. I believe now that his kind stop at nothing to get what they want. *Kilunewak wingi*! They are given to lying."

Khamseen agreed. He remembered his own feelings of hatred when he saw the detestable Kendall with Akayna. "We cannot let him see Akayna. He may try to kidnap her again," Khamseen said. "He thinks she belongs to the Englishman, Sir Aidan. Did I tell you how she outwitted him?"

He told his host the whole story of Akayna's confrontation with Kendall and Sir Aidan on the island of Funchal. How she tricked them into believing that she had been sexually intimate with him.

Anesquam looked at him with raised eyebrows. "So," he said questioningly, "you have not gone between my daughter's legs to take her maidenhood?"

The response from the African came quickly. "Not I, nor any other. She is as she left your home; flawless, unharmed... and pure."

He bowed his head in agreement when the Indian chief said, wonder showing in his tone, "You are a most unusual man."

Conceitedly, Khamseen agreed inwardly with the chief's assessment of him. He, a black man, had accomplished what he had set out to do. Against all odds, he had rescued a stolen maiden, stolen a rich man's boat, charted and sailed almost unknown seas, survived a mutiny, a devastating hurricane, and overcome the most difficult of all situations... restrained himself from physical contact with the woman he wanted.

Was the moment he had yearned for now at hand? Could he speak to this Indian chief, a man from another race and culture? Dare he verbalize to another person what he wanted?

He heard Ibraha's voice from the night before, *"Speak soon, or it may be too late."*

"I must reward you for all that you have done," Anesquam continued. "We of the Algonquin nation believe that when one has distinguished oneself as you have, to overcome obstacles and difficulties, to put self aside to care for another not even of his kind, that person must be honored. It will be discussed with the elders this evening."

"Sir, I have waited long for this moment to return a fledgling to the nest. I pray now that you do not look only at the color of my skin, but see beneath the outer covering to my heart, soul and brain. I love your daughter and I plead for her hand in marriage."

The Indian chief saw the earnest flush that crept beneath the man's dark skin. He sensed the intensity of the African's emotions. He, too, struggled with his own feelings... so much had happened, and the next few weeks were going to be critical ones for his tribe. There were serious problems with the "Yengees," the phonetic pronunciation of "English" by the Algonquins. Years later, others would translate it as "Yankees."

He sighed, rose, and turned to Khamseen, who also stood to face him. Both were tall men, but the Indian chief was a fraction shorter than his guest.

"It will be Akayna's decision, but you have my permission to speak to her."

Khamseen bowed respectfully and made the traditional salutation with his right hand placed first on his forehead, then on his heart.

CHAPTER FOURTEEN

The English colonists were still demanding land. More and more of them were arriving in the new world, swelling the population from Boston to the Providence Plantations in Rhode Island. The Indians were little match for the greed and fire power of the invaders — the ruthlessness they exhibited in their dealings with the natives, the diseases they brought, and the most dread of all, the introduction of *beson* liquor. Anesquam had even heard of another island on which the Dutch had landed. The Indians called it *Manahachtanienk*, which in the language of that tribe meant "The island where we all got drunk." It was almost a prophesy that some-day the island of Manhattan would become such a place — of drink, revelry and many cultures crowded onto it.

It had come to Anesquam's attention that the English were really outnumbering his tribesmen. The tribe was being pushed out of their homeland and forced deeper into the woods and nearby swamp lands. Their regular hunting of deer, fox, rabbit and squirrel had become more difficult. The English forgot the treaties they had signed and showed utter disdain for the native popula-tion.

Anesquam was heartsick over his inability to lead and protect his people. He was beginning to think that the settlers did not see his people as humans. It was evident in the injustices forced on the natives — land confiscation, all types of cheating practices, and rejection of the natives' beliefs. The Indians that had remained near the English villages had died from the diseases they had no natural immunity for, and many infants and small children had succumbed to whooping cough, measles, smallpox and dysentery. Anesquam knew he had to act. The tribal council met that evening.

• • •

Khamseen had returned to the ship right after the ceremonial meal had ended. He was not aware that the *Sea Treasure* had been noticed by the greedy settlers. When he boarded the ship, Ibraha told him about the difficulty he had in keeping a party from boarding. He told Khamseen how he had lied and said there was sickness aboard to keep the would-be pirates at bay.

"Khamseen, we must leave this place. They will be back, you know. They'll stop at nothing to steal this vessel. We must pull anchor and leave."

"I can't. Akayna's father, the chief, has given me permission to speak to Akayna."

"Where is she now?" Ibraha asked.

"The women have taken her away for a purification ceremony."

"You spoke to her father?" Ibraha asked, trying to keep the anxiety out of his voice.

"I did, Ibraha, and he has given me permission to speak with her. But, he says, the decision will be hers to make."

Ibraha's heart almost stopped. The decision would

be Akayna's. Was there hope for him?

• • •

The reports at the council meeting that evening were very bad. More and more sorrow was heaped on the sachem's heart.

Winter Bear, one of his trusted friends, reported that the widow, Sleeps-in-the-Woods, had found several settlers' cows grazing placidly in her cornfield. "Like they had every right to be there," she said. When she tried to move them out, a settler came at her with a "shooting stick."

Then, to make matters worse, the same man came to her with a piece of paper with marks on it. He said Sleeps-in-the-Woods' young son had signed the paper giving the settler permission to graze his cattle on her land. This was denied by Sleeps-in-the-Woods' son, Gray Hare. He did admit that the Yengee had given him spirit water. He did not remember ever signing with a crossmark any paper, however.

Black Snake, another chieftain, reported to the council that a white settler told him that because he was only an Indian, the laws from the white father in England said he, as a Yengee, could take whatever he needed. Black Snake said the man pulled down his *wetu* and built a wooden house of his own on the very spot. To make matters worse, Black Snake told the council, "This is the evil one who admitted to the killing of the white child, Ella Gardner. He said he was only trying to fondle her when she struggled, fell back on a rock, and struck her head."

"And because of his lying, my beloved daughter was banished from her home!" Anesquam said scornfully. "There are too many of them here! The land cannot care for so many mouths," Anesquam said.

"Aye," Black Snake agreed. "*Machelook*, many white people."

From the back of the long house, a muttering could be heard. Anesquam knew he would have to act — somehow drive the intruders from their land.

"*Yuh gachtonalatam!* Let us attack them!" The words were repeated from the back of the room to the front. The sound grew in intensity. Anesquam, weary of the struggle, faced the inevitable. They could not stand by helplessly while the invaders kept stealing their land, their food, their lives.

Slowly, Anesquam stood. The raging voices grew quiet. Even as a "praying" Indian, he recognized the outer limits of his control. The signed treaties were meaningless because the Yengees did not abide by them.

Anesquam raised his hand for silence. The council waited. He looked each man directly in the eyes, determining each man's intent. The room was death-like in its silence. He saw agreement. Anesquam stood erect. His sallow skin seemed even paler in the flicker of the camp fire situated in the middle of the room. It was rare for an Indian to perspire, but those close to the sachem could see beads of moisture on his upper lip.

"I see a black cloud has arisen yonder," he said soberly. The rivers will run with blood — ours and theirs. The Yengees speak with their lips only, not their hearts. We have not even room to spread our own blankets. I have heard your words," he again looked around the room, "and they have penetrated my heart. We will leave this place for safer ground."

CHAPTER FIFTEEN

To Akayna, the world seemed washed clean and new as she walked with her father to their favorite spot, a fallen oak tree. It was on a small rise that overlooked the village. Early morning frost had deposited sparkling jewels of water on the grass, and the brook that lay beyond the grassy slope to the rear of Anesquam's long house moved energetically as its rain-swollen boundaries threatened to rise over its banks.

Wordlessly, father and daughter moved in unison to their remembered area. Many important conversations had taken place there between the two. Akayna took deep breaths of the sweet air, welcomed it into her lungs, and then she exhaled forcefully. She was happy to be home. When her father had suggested that they take a walk after their morning meal of maize and last evening's warmed over soup, Akayna's intuition warned her, as happy as she felt, that this talk would be of a serious nature.

As tradition dictated, the daughter waited respectfully for her father to speak first.

"There goes Winter Bear's eldest son, Yellow Bear," he said, pointing to a young man moving into the woods behind them. "He is out early to hunt, I think. Do you know," her father continued as they watched the man and his dog, "he has trained that dog, using silent commands, to hunt? He only has to motion with his hand or his head and his dog knows just what to do — when to point, when to fetch. Yellow Bear has taught his animal well. He's a smart lad; brings honor to his family. Has the makings of a good hunter and a fine warrior."

"I see. Father," Akayna asked thoughtfully, looking at her father's strong hands as they rested on his knees, "are you sorry that..." she hesitated slightly, "that you do not have a son? That I am a girl?"

Her father turned on the log to face her. He spoke quietly. "My seed was planted into your mother with all the love I had to give. When the time was ripe, you came, a lovely human being formed by your mother and me and the Great Spirit."

With his forefinger, Anesquam traced a soft caress around his daughter's face. "I thought I would die when I had to send you away from me. Child, never in this life have I received a greater gift than you."

Love for her father flooded Akayna, and she impulsively pressed her head on her father's chest. His shoulder cape of iridescent turkey feathers interwoven with soft down felt soothing and comforting to her face. She could feel the warmth from her father's body, and she was aware of the reassuring thump of his heart. She was secure and safe — at last.

"Oh Father, I've missed you so. I thought I'd never see you again. That wicked Henry Kendall, his filthy boat, the raging waters of the seas, all the horrible days and nights — so many places, so many people, the cities! Father, I did not know Mother Earth was so big, and never have I been more frightened."

Anesquam smiled and hugged her close for a brief moment, a rare gesture for an Algonquin. "You have much to speak of, daughter, during *Hawkswawney,* our storytelling time, I guess, after all your many travels."

"I do, Father. Some of it I find hard to believe really happened to me. Now that I am home, it seems to be a dream."

"Much has happened here in our village as well."

"Father, I heard you thank the Great Spirit for my return. Are you still a 'praying' Indian?"

"Aha, my child, you noticed. Before, I thought if I declared to believe in the English God, we would all live together on this land as a peaceful community. My judgment was wrong. You know, the one that killed Ella Gardner was found, but his law said her killing was only an accident; no malice was behind his act. So he received no punishment whatever! What kind of god is that, to allow no punishment for such a dastardly deed? Even you, my child, were made to suffer! I could not remain a 'praying' Indian. There have been many wrongs done to our people since you were forced into exile."

"It has been bad for our people?"

"I can hardly find the words to pass over my lips to tell you how bad. Widows have lost their lands, the young men of the tribe have been seduced by that evil *beson,* liquor. It burns their throats and clouds their minds, so they do not even know their own mothers.

"What do you plan to do, Father?"

"We will leave this place," her father said, his face clouded over with dismay. "But, daughter," he took

Akayna's hand in his, "now I must speak to you about the man who returned you to me."

Akayna felt a momentary pang of alarm. She noticed the solemn expression in her father's face. She knew she could be affected by his next words. "Yes Father, Khamseen."

"He intends to ask you to marry him."

"Marry him?"

"He has already asked me."

"What... what did you say?"

"I told him that I knew you owed him your life. I told him I would ask you to consider. I told him the decision, however, was yours."

Akayna knew why her father would allow Khamseen to speak. The Algonquin nation, of which her tribe, the Wampanoag, was a part, believed that any good deed did not go unrewarded. She knew also that her father would see it as his duty to honor the claim of one that had performed so admirably in his daughter's behalf. What *did* she feel for Khamseen? He had always been kind, considerate, and seemed to want to please her. But there was something else as well. Deep in her mind, she always felt that she was not the sole reason Khamseen had undertaken his incredible voyage. She had overheard some of his conversations with Ibraha while on the ship. Khamseen had said more than once, *"One dares to do the impossible because others say it cannot be done. That is the challenge — to do the impossible."* Perhaps this whole adventure was just his personal challenge. To outwit his enemies, cross a new ocean, come unscathed through mutiny and hurricane, even, perhaps, rescue an unknown stranger.

Akayna remembered the rakish grin he would display when he had won an argument, scored a point, or bested an opponent. It was almost as if with a shrug of his shoulders he was saying, *"I can't help it if I am clever! It was meant to be."* His confidence was smug and sure.

She knew that it was his intention to return to his home, no longer just an apprentice shipbuilder, but a wealthy adventurer of African descent to be reckoned with. She saw in Khamseen a selfish ego, a vanity that somehow irritated her. She had seen his tendency to push... to force others to do his will. There was a distinction between vanity and pride. Khamseen had gambled; defied the emir by stealing his ship. He had risked the lives of many to do what he said he could do. Now, it seemed, to cap all of his feats he wished to marry the sachem's daughter. But she knew that she did not love him.

The thoughts swirled around in Akayna's head and she realized her father was waiting for her response. "I know, Father, that our tribal code says I owe Khamseen. But I do not want this man. I do not love him. I am sincerely grateful to him, but is gratitude sufficient for marriage?"

"Daughter, he deserves consideration. He has saved your life. As the daughter of the chief sachem, you must honor his deed. It cannot go unrewarded."

Akayna bowed her head at her father's words. "I will consider it," she said.

As father and daughter walked back to the *wetu*, each was engrossed in deep thought. Akayna knew her father's concern was the future of the tribe... the inevitable confrontation with the ever-encroaching, aggressive Yengees.

Her thoughts reeled with her father's words, *"You must honor his deed. It cannot go unrewarded."* Somehow she was repulsed by the idea of marriage to the, as she saw him, selfish Khamseen. And she was wearied by having her life's decisions dictated by others. She would make her own decisions, or why live at all? She'd rather die than marry someone out of gratitude or honor; no matter the Wampanoag tradition. After all, she was a sachem's daughter, wasn't she?

And in the back of her mind and her heart lay the face of Ibraha. She had not forgotten that moonlit night on the *Sea Treasure*, nor the feel of Ibraha's mouth on her yielding lips. What did it all mean?

CHAPTER SIXTEEN

The very next morning, Akayna looked for one of the natives who had brought her ashore the day before. "Can you take me back to the ship? I must get some of my belongings that I left on board."

"You know, my lady," he spoke in a sober tone, "they say there is sickness on that ship. Should you go back?"

His hesitation angered Akayna. "Of course I should. If there is sickness on board, I have already been exposed to it. Do I look sick to you?" She glared at him.

"No, no, my lady," he shook his head, and led her to the small canoe. He rowed her out to the *Sea Treasure,* anchored about one-half mile from shore, and was instructed to return for her an hour before sunset.

It was a beautiful bright day. The sky's blueness was enhanced by lace-like wisps of white clouds that danced joyously across the horizon. Despite the beauty of the day, Akayna's thoughts were troubling to her. Her father's admonition that she give Khamseen's request consideration bothered her. She would never willingly hurt her father, but was it wrong to have a different viewpoint? She thought of her travels, her forced exile from her father's home, being kidnapped from Sir Aidan's villa, meeting people of different colors and nations. She remembered the sadistic cruelty of Henry Kendall, the weakness she saw in Sir Aidan, the sympathy she received from his maid, Mistress Cooley — all different people. As she sat in the small canoe, she realized that unlike her father, her world had widened far beyond her father's or her own imagination. What she had seen and felt during the past weeks had changed her from an innocent Indian girl to a young woman on the threshold of her adult life. Was she seeking an answer to her dilemma; was that why she had come out to the ship? Would she find her answer there? She wondered.

Ibraha was at the wheel of the ship and he quickly let down a rope ladder when he recognized Akayna seated in the front of the native's canoe.

"I had to come back, Ibraha," she said breathlessly as she stepped on the deck. "I had to come to get Panseis and the baskets that I made. And I did want to say good-bye to Zaid and the others." She did not voice the other reasons that were in her mind.

"Khamseen is not here," Ibraha said.

"Not here?" Akayna's eyes widened at the news.

"He left early this morning to go to the English village of Monset to trade guns."

Akayna gasped, horrified, and pressed her hands to her chest. "Then he does not know that my father and the tribal council may declare war against the Yengees. He could be in danger."

"I warned him not to go, but Khamseen..."

"Saw it as a challenge, I know," she interrupted.

Ibraha heard a certain amount of disdain in her voice.

"Khamseen has always been a trader," Ibraha said. "He has never hesitated to try to make a profit. I think it's in his blood, to barter and trade like his grandfather, the African who sold brass and leather goods in the *souks* in Morocco.

"I knew Khamseen had arms to sell. I saw them brought on board in Barbados. But why must he sell to the Yengees? Why not to *my* people. They need 'shooting sticks'."

Ibraha shrugged his shoulders. "I learned long ago not to interfere with anything Khamseen wanted to do. I offer advice, but that is all. Khamseen is ambitious, single-minded and determined. He wants to be wealthy and successful. That is an admirable goal, Akayna, to acquire wealth and status."

"Well, perhaps," she answered grudgingly, "but I think Khamseen believes my people to be weak. They are not, and he doesn't know the Yengees here as we do."

"What do you mean, Akayna?"

"It's been over twenty years since the English first came to our shores. My father asked some of them 'Why you come here?' The Vikings and others came to fish, then they left, but the English said they were looking for a 'fresh new place'. We, my father and the elders, thought they meant firewood."

"You did not know they had left their country because of religious beliefs?"

"No, all we knew, my father has said, is that they wanted what we had — our land."

As they walked toward the companionway to go below deck, Akayna greeted several of the crew who were busily cleaning and polishing the deck and rails.

She looked for Zaid. She had particularly wanted to say good-bye to her young friend. She was disappointed. She asked, "And Zaid, he is with Khamseen?"

"Yes, he went along with him. You know how much the lad admires Khamseen. Do you think they will be safe?" Ibraha worried.

"I really don't know, Ibraha. I do not trust the English. My father did once; he tried as a 'praying' Indian, but now..." her voice trailed off into silence.

They continued down the steps onto the lower deck. Suddenly, Akayna became acutely aware of Ibraha's presence. She felt an unmistakable magnetism flow from him. It was as if a fiery current flashed through her body. She stumbled and Ibraha took hold of her arm to steady her. There was a sudden rise in her own body temperature from the contact with his strong hand. She glanced quickly at him and noticed a deep flush under his dark skin.

Intuitively, Akayna realized that somehow, this time, she had moved into a questionable zone. She was not unaware of Ibraha's feelings toward her. Many times since that fateful day in Funchal she had sensed his support, his deep concern for her welfare, the symbolic gift of Panseis. In the recesses of her mind, she wondered about her immediate future. From her earliest childhood her mother, Monticut, had taught her to look for little signs; *"Notice changes in the eyes of a person,"* she had said. *"The smallest body movements, the nerves, the sounds and tones of the voice, the tiniest manifestations can speak louder than any words."* Akayna had learned her lessons well and she knew Ibraha was attracted to her. And she had not forgotten that kiss on the moonlit ship. Again, the memory arose in her mind.

She knew, too, that it was rare for an Indian woman to break away from the traditional role assigned to her. But she was aware that in her tribal culture the sexes were considered equal. If she *did* deviate from the ordinary, but could hold her own against all odds, she would continue to be held in high regard.

The thought of having to marry Khamseen out of gratitude rankled within her, gave her the feeling of *schwan*, a sharp, bitter taste in her mouth. How could he assume that because of what he had done, she would feel obligated to him? And knowing that he had gone to sell arms to the Yengees deepened her dislike for him. One thing she did know — good and evil could not dwell in the same heart. Not even Khamseen's heart.

She felt herself moving to a different path. And it was not the path chosen for her. Unwittingly, *she* had chosen the path by returning to the ship.

• • •

Ibraha could hardly believe that Akayna was standing beside him in the small salon of the *Sea Treasure*, the room that had been her bedroom. How many times had he ached to be near her? How many nights had he dreamed of her in his arms, only to awaken to frustrating emptiness? He wondered briefly if Khamseen had spoken to her of marriage. Had she agreed?

As he watched her gather the baskets she had made, some colorfully decorated with birds and butterflies, he could not help but notice the easy grace with which she moved. It was as if the bones inside her skin were weightless. Her simple Indian deerskin shift fell from a drawstring tied at her neckline. Her twin braids had been coiled in a crown fashion and gave her a regal appearance. Her legs were covered with white fringed leather leggings to her knees. Her beaded moccasins were made of white leather as well. She wore a turquoise and silver necklace, and there were tiny chips of turquoise in her ears.

When Akayna finished gathering her belongings, she turned to face him. Ibraha's heart almost stopped. Never in all his years had a woman been so appealing to him. And never one more beautiful and desirable than this one standing before him. Thoughts of disloyalty to Khamseen, thoughts of betrayal, of breaking a bond, filled his mind. He, Ibraha, wanted a woman desired by his friend. He had been Khamseen's confidante; shared problems with him, sailed an almost unknown sea with him, fought the same enemies. But still, at this moment, if he dared listen to his heart, he would never share his life with Khamseen again. Akayna, the sachem's daughter, had altered their lives forever. He could wait no longer.

"Akayna," Ibraha's voice broke as he spoke her name. He held his arms open.

Akayna blinked at the sight of the tall man whose skin was as black as a velvet night, a clear, glowing, jet-black; whose deep brown eyes looked at her with tenderness. She saw a proud man of another race, from a faraway land in the world that she had never before dreamed existed. She sensed his desire for her. Sensed his will pull her toward him as he waited, expectantly. Nothing mattered anymore. She knew the place she wanted to be. Something had led her to this. Perhaps, just perhaps, she had set out, as if drawn by an unknown force, to find Ibraha.

"Ibraha," she said, as she moved into his arms.

Ibraha tilted her face up toward his as he bent to kiss her. The sweetness of the gentle caress as his lips touched hers unbalanced her and she pulled him closer, holding him tightly. It was the ageless need of a woman for the man she loves.

Strong waves of passion overtook Ibraha as he tasted the honey-like nectar of Akayna's lips. He moaned, abandoning all constraints. She had come to him this day.

Akayna did not know what to expect next, but she knew there would be no turning back. She had to satisfy the aching core of her being, and that could only be fulfilled by the strong, gentle African who held her. His soft breath in her ear made her legs quiver. She could not stand, even with Ibraha's arms around her. He sensed her weakness and picked her up before her knees crumpled. Gently, he placed her on the narrow bed.

"You are safe here, my love," Ibraha breathed into her ear. The soft breath fluttered, tantalizing her ears. She turned her eyes to look into his. "We belong to each other. You know we do," he murmured. "Kiss me, my love," Ibraha said as he brushed her lips gently with his own.

Akayna, hungry for the fulfillment of the desire she was experiencing, remained mute as Ibraha pulled the coronet of braids from the top of her head. Using his fingers, he untwined the thick braids until her hair fell in a dusky, mysterious curtain about her face.

With the experience of many loves, Ibraha gently began to trace soft kisses around Akayna's face and neck. She closed her eyes to savor the glory of his light caresses, and he continued to kiss her closed eyelids, his large, capable hands clasped into her hair. Akayna trembled with her own growing desire. She had no idea she would behave this way. She was almost frightened by the behavior of her body. As Ibraha continued to trace a path of kisses to the hollow of her neck, she began to murmur and moan. She felt Ibraha loosen the drawstring that tied her shift around her neck. He pulled down the top of the deerskin dress and exposed her tawny shoulders. Her breasts were freed from their restraints and Ibraha's firm fingers circled the golden orbs tenderly and teased them into throbbing centers of sensuality.

"Please, Akayna, let me love you." Ibraha's voice was husky and persistent as his mouth replaced his fingers. Akayna felt a fire leap within her body as she instinctively cradled the dark head to her bosom.

Suddenly, Ibraha got to his feet and gently pulled her shift to her knees. He released the leggings and soon her naked body lay ready before his hungry eyes as he stripped himself of his clothing.

His dark eyes devoured her. Never had he seen a body more perfect, more beautiful. His breath was taken by the vision of Akayna's long, slender legs, invitingly lovely hips and her fully developed, exquisitely-formed breasts, each peaked with a delicate bud. Her blue-black hair lay like a gossamer veil around her face and shoulders. Her face was shining and damp, flushed with emotion as her dark eyes watched him.

He knelt on the floor beside the narrow bed. "Don't be afraid, little one," he crooned softly. "You are so lovely and I want you so much. You are a beautiful bird from paradise; you must have come from the heavens."

As the ship rocked back and forth on the gentle waters of Cape Cod, Ibraha touched her beautiful, elegant skin with gentle kisses. His lips, moist with love, slid over her body as he traced a loving path over every inch of her skin. She arched her body with the excitement, and Ibraha was delighted when he saw her sooty eyes search his face. Her high cheekbones were luminous with desire and her lips were parted as her breath panted jerkily through her lips. It was as if her soul was soaring away from her as Ibraha touched her enchanting body with his tongue. Her stomach muscles quivered as his moist lips and tongue slipped over her belly. Her long thighs parted and her toes curled involuntarily as the tension increased.

He lay over her then; his lean, supple body felt both hot and cool as his skin lovingly touched hers. Ibraha could feel Akayna's heart fluttering beneath his hand. She moaned greedily as she held Ibraha's head to her breast. The contact of his body with hers urged her own body to action, and he sensed the hunger she had felt for the past months. The longing, the feelings of abandonment began to peel away as Ibraha gently caressed and loved her. She rose to his fingers' delicate probings and welcomed him to the tender secret spot that he ached to find. He knew then that she was his and his alone.

They left the ship later that day and Akayna took Ibraha to her favorite spot in the woods.

"My father has changed so much, Ibraha. He is not the same man I left here."

Ibraha took her face in his hands and shook his head slowly as he peered into her sorrowful eyes. I want you to know that I love you, and as soon as I can settle things I will help you. I cannot do otherwise."

"But what if Khamseen insists on your returning

with him?"

"He may try, but he was the one who stole the ship. I came with him because I promised his father... but then, even if I had not wanted to make the voyage, once I saw you, light of my life, nothing, nothing could have made me turn back."

Ibraha pulled her close to him and she could hear the comforting beat of his heart.

It all sounded so simple, but what of *her* obligations?

CHAPTER SEVENTEEN

Akayna had noticed the increasingly greying pallor in her father's face. His once tall, straight figure was becoming more stooped, as if the burdens of caring for the tribe were almost more than he could tolerate. He had changed so much since the day he sent her away. She sent for the medicine man, the Keeper-of-the-Faith, to tend to her ailing parent. She trusted that he could help. Something had to be done. Her father seemed to be drying up, to have given up, and turned his face more often to the wall of the *wetu* as he lay on his cedar bark bed. Soon he stopped speaking, even to Akayna. Her heart ached. She realized that her father was dying. If he died, she'd have no one. A picture of Khamseen rose in her mind. Even if her father died, she still had to honor his obligations. And that could mean she'd have to marry Khamseen. How could she, when it was Ibraha she loved.

• • •

Soon after Anesquam's death, preparations were made for the burial ceremony. Anesquam's body was dressed in his chief's finery. A supple tanned deerskin, the hair side close to the body, had been tied at the waist by a deer tail. The deerskin was decorated with embroidery of colored woven plant fibers and seeds. A bear claw necklace, symbol of authority, was draped around the chief's neck, and there were rows of copper bracelets on both arms. A beautiful feather coronet around his forehead gave his quiet face a look of dignity. A lap robe of white moose skin covered the lower half of his body.

The Keeper-of-the-Faith, also the chief medicine man, had been appointed to his position by Akayna's maternal grandmother because such positions of authority were made by the matriarchs of the tribe. As befitted one with this power, the shaman would be responsible for the burial ceremony that was due Anesquam, a sachem, a man of respect.

As word of the tragedy swept through the campsite, men, women and children, their faces painted black in sorrow with soot and charcoal, cried and wailed aloud in unabashed grief. Unwiped tears streaked paths of white and gave their faces a bewitched, demonic appearance. As the tribe moved forward to pay their respects, their loud cries and moans filled the morning air.

Akayna respectfully bowed her head low before her father's body. She wept quietly, then turned as the elder women of the tribe took her in their arms and led her away. She would be prepared for the final farewell to her father.

The Keeper-of-the-Faith came to her long house later that afternoon to tell her that the burial ceremony was about to begin.

"Are his hands before his face?" she asked.

"It is so, my daughter," he replied. "He will face the

Great Spirit in a humble fashion."

"And has he been laid to rest on his right side so that he faces the east to see the first light?" she queried.

"It is also as you say. The bottom of the grave has been lined with soft branches and fir mats. His weapons of honor — tomahawk, quiver, bow, arrows and spear, are at his right side. I have ordered bowls of corn and dried meat, as well as his beloved *calumet,* the peace pipe, to be placed on his left side. All is in readiness for the weepers and mourners, and for you, to bid farewell to him."

• • •

Ibraha's heart was heavy with shared grief for Akayna. He knew that although Akayna had told Khamseen that she could not marry him because of her love for Ibraha, she still felt she must honor her obligations to him. He, too, was still torn between his desire for Akayna and his loyalty to Khamseen. Deep in his heart he knew what he wanted to do, but before he could do it he would have to free himself of all obligations to Khamseen. The new change in their relationship meant there could be no hope of returning to the symbiotic bonding they had once shared. Strangely enough, there did not seem to be any enmity between them, but more of a sadness, a troubled end to a once admirable relationship.

Ibraha knew, too, that he would not return to Morocco. Even if Akayna did not become a part of his life, he knew he would still remain in the new world. He would use what skills he had learned dealing with crew members, whaling, sailing, building boats, and he would acquire whatever other skills were necessary to make it in this place called America. He would not be too proud to say to anyone, Indian or settler, "I do not know, teach me." He would do what he needed to do to be near Akayna, the woman he loved.

• • •

As Khamseen and his men neared the *Sea Treasure* in the small canoe, the men noticed several young Indian boys on board. Too young to volunteer for fighting, they had been ecstatic when Akayna gave them the honor of guarding the *Sea Treasure*. When Khamseen boarded, he thanked the Indian boys for guarding the ship. He spoke to Ibraha as they inspected the ship. "I have nothing to give them," he said.

"I don't think they expect anything. Being out here in charge of a vessel gave them a great sense of honor and pride, I think," Ibraha said thoughtfully. "You can see the pride shining in their eyes. Indeed, Khamseen, from what I have seen of these people, they seem to want to protect us. They do not seem to have a nature toward conflict unless they are pushed to it."

"You seem to have taken to these people, Ibraha."

Khamseen stopped before moving down the companionway to inspect the lower deck. He looked directly at Ibraha for confirmation of his observation. Both men knew at that moment that the bond between them was broken. Khamseen waited for an answer from Ibraha, which he knew would make his own personal decision a right one for him. He would have no guilt about the selfish path he was planning to take.

"I think you know, Khamseen, as well as I do, that I am bound to stay here. I love Akayna and her people as well. Whatever future I have, I will find here."

"As you wish," Khamseen answered. "When do you want to leave the ship? Soon?" His eyebrows lifted up in twin question marks. He was anxious for Ibraha to be gone so he could be alone to search out his hiding place, retrieve what he had hidden, and prepare to sail. He would go to Virginia, to Portsmouth, and pick up cotton, tobacco, rum and other goods he could sell in Morocco.

He vowed he would be a rich man when he returned with the emir's boat. He was determined that he would not be a pauper, a beggar who had to plead for favors from the wealthy. From poor, humble beginnings, he would be rich, equal in wealth to any. And, he surmised, if he didn't get what he sought in Virginia or the Carolinas, he would return to the island of Barbados. He would surely be able to make a good living with the *Sea Treasure* there.

Now, knowing how it was between himself and Ibraha, he felt his decision not to tell Ibraha about his secret cache was the right one.

"Perhaps it would be good to return with the young men in the canoe," Ibraha said. He saw Khamseen straighten his body and stand tall. Ibraha sensed Khamseen's eagerness for him to leave. At last, Khamseen would be on his very own, and Ibraha was very aware of Khamseen's need for independence.

He gathered his belongings from his bunk, from the space he had shared with his former friend, and tied them into a bundle.

Khamseen spoke first, before he turned. "I wish you well, Ibraha."

"And I you." Ibraha ran back up the companionway and hailed the young Indians that were going down the ship's ladder.

Khamseen did not watch him leave. As soon as he

was sure that he was alone, that the crew was busy elsewhere on topside, he pulled on the bunk bed that he had slept in and pried it loose from the bulkhead of the ship. He took his knife and pressed along a wide seam. Then he pushed aside a space about three feet wide. On his knees, he crawled into the darkened interior until he found what he was searching for. It was there. Khamseen exulted inwardly. He would be a success. The gold coins he had hidden there were safe. He scrambled, crab-like, backward into the room. He replaced the board, sealed the wall and pushed back the bunk. No one would be using the cabin but him.

He dashed up to the foredeck to instruct the crew. "Up anchor! Look to the sails, belay there, fasten the ropes! Hurry, we must be underway before any trouble comes!"

The crew jumped to his commands, and only as the *Sea Treasure* began to move on the tide did Khamseen look toward the shoreline. He could see nothing except a sandy beach and an empty canoe pulled in under the trees. He turned his face to the sea, but his mind was on an Indian beauty for whom he had risked life, limb and reputation. He was not satisfied at all with the turn of events. He would not give her up, however. He still had the ship and he would find a cargo to take back to the emir. And he would outwit Ibraha and have Akayna.

CHAPTER EIGHTEEN

After the last spade of earth was placed on Anesquam's grave, his followers piled stones over it to keep marauding animals from uncovering the corpse. Then they returned to his *wetu*. A large stone from Anesquam's hearth, the ceramic stone bowl he used for his evening meal, and one of his spears were all placed together in front of his home. They would remain there until they became fragments. No one would disturb them because to do so would mean that Anesquam's spirit would wander the earth, unable to find comfort.

Later that same evening, the Keeper-of-the-Faith came to the dead chief's *wetu*. He carried with him a flaming torch. The other members of the tribe gathered as well, still wailing and mourning. Their cries rose into a crescendo of sorrow as the shaman walked the perimeter of the home, touching various areas with the torch. As the crackling flames arose, the crowd's cries and moans became louder and louder. The roaring blaze, mingled with the cacophony of grieving voices, created a diorama of sadness; fear mixed with a sense of finality and cleanliness as the flames fell into ashes. It was done. Anesquam was no more. His name would never again be mentioned. He was free to find his way to the kind winds of the Great Spirit, *Kautantowwit*.

Akayna watched silently. She stood alone, sentinel-like, waiting until, hours later, the last red ember glowed and faded to a gray, lifeless ash. Now she was truly an orphan. There had not been time to share with her father the many stories she had meant to tell him — the treachery of Henry Kendall, the extraordinary ocean voyages, the people she had met in Torremolinos, in Funchal, Barbados, and most importantly, the duplicity of Khamseen and the passion she felt for the other African, Ibraha. Now even he was gone. Where was he? Would she ever see him again? She blinked away her tears when the shaman touched her elbow.

"My lady," he bowed graciously, "you have been named squaw sachem. It has been decided by the Council of Mothers. The ceremony will be held in three days' time. The women wait."

Akayna turned her back to the pile of ashes that was once home and noticed the group of older women, their faces still blackened. Some she recognized as friends of her mother, one was her aunt, her father's sister, and an older one was her grandmother's youngest sister. This group of women owned most of the land and goods of the tribe. When the men went to war, or off to hunt and fish, it was the women who became self-sufficient and independent. Because they controlled the economy, they controlled the tribe. They had even selected the Keeper-of-the-Faith, and had seen to his training and education as a shaman.

The women circled Akayna and led her to the sweat room. She was stripped of her clothing and placed within the stone circular hut. It was just high enough for her to stand. The stones on the floor in a center pile had been heated for some time. Then cool water was poured over them to create a heavy steam. For an hour, Akayna sat on a wooden plank while the sweat poured in great rivulets from her slender body. She became languid and dream-like, and she thought she heard Ibraha's deep voice. *"Come to me, my beloved, let me place my love around you and hold you close. Come to me."*

Akayna moaned, her mind in turmoil from the worry and trauma she had experienced. It seemed to her that her life had been moving in a confused kaleidoscopic pattern. When would it make sense and be real for her again?

The flap of the stone hut was opened from the outside and cool refreshing air rushed in. Still drowsy, Akayna felt a deerskin, soft and smooth, being draped over her naked body as she was led to the next step of the purification ceremony. She walked dream-like on the pine needle carpeted path to the stream's edge where she was pushed, gasping, into the cold waters of the brook.

Stunned and shocked, Akayna swam quickly to the other side of the stream. She knew she had to do it or she would not be allowed to become the squaw sachem. *I do owe that to my father,* she thought, as she scrambled up the wooded bank of the stream.

"Come, daughter." Her grandmother's sister, Suquktoh, held out a cloak made of woven fibers and took Akayna into her *wetu*. She handed the girl a cup of herb tea which Akayna gulped down and reached for another. Her thirst was overwhelming, but her nerves were beginning to quiet down a little and she was happy to be with her grandmother's sister.

"Aunt, will I be a proper squaw sachem?" she asked, as the older woman dried her long black hair.

"Of course, child. We mothers of the tribe selected the one before you and we have selected you to follow. His blood runs in your veins, and you will lead our people as a true sachem."

A small fire flickered on the tiny hearth in her great-aunt's *wetu* and Akayna felt pangs of hunger, but she knew there would be only water for her until after the ceremony. She had three days to fast, and on the third night she would become her tribe's leader. Until that time, she would remain in the small *wetu* to fast and pray to the Great Spirit for guidance. Her only human companion would be her elderly great-aunt, who would visit her at sunrise and sunset. At sunset, the old woman left, and Akayna fell into a fitful sleep.

The next morning, when the old woman came, she questioned Akayna. "Daughter, have you cleared your mind for the future?" she asked Akayna.

"Aunt, I know that I should. I had so many...," she couldn't speak her dead father's name, "so many things, so many places I wanted to tell about at *Hawkswawney*, but now those days are past and seem as if they almost did not happen."

"Perhaps you should forget them and put them in your past." The old Indian woman was tiny and rather wrinkled, but her face held a warmth and kindness that comforted Akayna.

When Akayna's great-aunt returned that same night, bringing more fresh water in a clay pot with a clay cup for Akayna to drink from, she decided that this sunset hour would be the time to ask about the problem she had not been able to settle with her father. It would have to be concluded in her mind before she could move ahead in her life. "Aunt," she began.

The ancient woman sat on the ground of the hut, stirred the hearth fire and threw on a few more twigs. She rummaged around the small hemp pouch she wore around her waist, extracted a clay pipe and some crushed tobacco leaves. After she had filled the pipe bowl, tamped down the tobacco with a bony finger, she reached for a lighted twig and placed it on the pipe bowl. She drew forcefully until the smoke began to rise and wreathe around her lank braids. "Speak, daughter. I can listen until the sun goes down. Then I must leave until the sun rises tomorrow."

"I know," Akayna said. "Aunt, the African, Khamseen," she began. "brought me back home. He rescued me from a traitor's trap, saved me from death and returned me to my home. I know what he has done is not to be considered lightly. I told him many times over that my..." she could not say *father's*, "that he would be paid for his trouble, but he does not want to be repaid with wampum. He wants to take me as his wife, back to his own home."

The aunt pulled on the pipe, squinting through the haze of smoke at the troubled girl. "The Algonquin way is to repay a debt of kindness when care and kindness have been given. You must consider this and the code of honor of our tribe must be upheld. You cannot become squaw sachem, otherwise."

"But Aunt, I cannot marry Khamseen. I do not love him. I love the other African, Ibraha."

"That changes things, but very little," the old woman said. "You must pray hard to the Great Spirit to guide you." She rose from her position on the floor, dusted off the back of her deerskin shift and went to the doorway of the small hut. "The sun has gone to bed. I can stay no longer. Pray this night," she said as she lowered the skin flap of the doorway and left.

Akayna drank some of the water, but she was extremely hungry. She had one more day of fasting before she would be taken before the Keeper-of-the-Faith who would complete the ceremony that would make her the squaw sachem.

She washed her face and arms and tied her hair into a single braid. In the quiet night, her thoughts turned to Ibraha. Where was he? Had he and Khamseen returned to Spain? *Put the thought of Ibraha aside,* she told herself. *You must pray for guidance.* Her stomach, without food for two days, rumbled and groaned. She tried to ignore the discomfort, and pulled her knees to her chest as she lay on a mat on the dirt floor.

Great Spirit, she prayed silently, *I am Akayna, your child. Breathe into my brain the message you would have me know to make my life a true one in your honor. I surrender to your will.*

CHAPTER NINETEEN

"Tonight," her great-aunt announced when she came with fresh water to Akayna's isolation hut, "tonight you will be made our new sachem."

"If my answers to your questions are true and worthy to your ears," Akayna answered.

The old woman grunted and painfully lowered herself to the dirt floor. She sat cross-legged in front of Akayna and rested her bony, gnarled fingers on her knees. She was ninety-three years old. Her eyes were sharp and piercing as she looked directly at her niece, as if searching the girl's face for truth.

After a few moments she began to ask her questions, speaking slowly.

"Did you make a request of the African, Khamseen, that he return you to your home?"

"I did not request it. I merely stated that I wanted to return home."

"Did you ever speak an untruth to him?"

"I never spoke an untruth to him."

"Did you lead him to believe that you wanted to marry him?"

"No, I did not lead him to believe I wanted to marry

him."

"Hmmm," the old woman grunted again. Then she cleared her throat before she spoke.

Akayna waited, expectantly.

"Did you give yourself to the man, Khamseen?"

"I never gave myself to the man, Khamseen," Akayna replied. Her mind flashed back to the ship and Ibraha as she thought of their lovemaking. She realized her great-aunt was still speaking, so she brought herself back to the present. This time her aunt's tone seemed less serious.

"Did you send some of our young men to protect the African's ship in the harbor from being seized by the Yengees?"

"Yes."

"Did you tell them to protect it with their lives?"

"Yes, I did."

The old woman got up from her position on the floor, dusted off the back of her shift, and placed her hand on Akayna's head almost in benediction. "My child, do not worry. You have repaid the debt. You saved the African's ship, which is his livelihood. I must leave now; the sun has risen. I will return at sunset."

• • •

During that last day of isolation, Akayna slept in brief naps. Her body was in distress from lack of food and she found herself almost too dizzy to stand. Her short naps were filled with visions of disembodied beings and animals, and she heard voices clamoring for her attention. She thought she saw her grandmother, Nookomebsa, her long gray hair streaming down her shoulders as she pointed a finger toward the west as if giving a direction to Akayna. She dreamed of her father who did not speak, merely offered her a warm, loving smile. She woke up with a cry when she realized that her lover, Ibraha, was also in the dream. He seemed to be pushing his way thorough a crowd, trying to reach her. When she woke, her face was wet with tears. *What is ahead for me?* she wondered.

Later that day, after the sun had lowered itself in the western sky, the Council of Mothers came to the isolation hut. Her mother's sister, Noni, noted how thin Akayna had become. She pressed her niece's head to her ample breast with the promise, "Your ordeal is almost over. Soon you will be our new sachem." She tried to sound cheerful, but she knew the girl would face many problems when she became the tribe's new leader.

Silently, the women began their task of preparing Akayna for her ceremony. She was given a warm bath, the water scented with herbs, and her hair was braided into a single braid that was wound crown-like around her head.

Soft white deerskin leggings, fringed with colored lacings and ties, were placed on her legs. A short underskirt of linen fiber was settled over her hips, and a long mantle made of two deerskins stitched together was put on over the underskirt. It was secured with a leather belt. Her moccasins were white with colorful beads embroidered on the toes and instep. The women worked in a smooth fashion; each one completed her assignment before passing Akayna on to the next woman.

A band of purple and white beaded wampum was put around Akayna's slender neck, and glinting copper earrings in her ears. She wore an amulet of wampum on each arm and a copper bracelet on each wrist. The wampum and copper were a sign of her family's wealth.

A rim of black pigment placed more focus on her lovely dark brown eyes, and a slight hint of red pigment, a sign of her royalty, was put on her cheeks. Before she was led out to the expectant crowd, a helmet of colorful pheasant feathers encircled her head. She looked regal and serene, but inwardly she felt weak and filled with apprehension. She thought of her father and vowed to herself to be a worthy successor to him.

She walked with her entourage from the isolation hut to the ceremonial lodge. Along the pathway, men, women and children watched silently as the lighted procession made its way to the site. No sound came from the onlookers. That would come later, after the shaman had pronounced Akayna squaw sachem.

The Keeper-of-the-Faith, shaman, medicine man — he was known by all those titles — met the group at the open door of the ceremonial lodge, a bark-domed, mat-sided building about sixty feet in diameter. He wore a turtle shell breastplate, Akayna's family clan. The Wampanoags were the turtle clan. On his head several large turkey feathers had been woven into his hair. He carried on his waist a leather medicine bag containing stone images of the Great Spirit, *Manitou*, as well as a pair of bells and a wooden flute, all instruments of his magic and power.

He spoke to Akayna.

"You are allowed one witness to enter this sacred house with you. Please choose."

Akayna turned to look at the covey of women who had loved and cared for her. She nodded to her grandmother's sister, the remaining member of her father's family. "I choose my honorable great-aunt," she said.

The man nodded in agreement. Slowly the three entered the large hut. The skin flap fell closed behind them.

First the shaman danced around the fire that burned in the center of the lodge. Then, after he had circled the fire ten times, he took his ceremonial pipe from his waistband, filled it with tobacco, and exhaled tobacco smoke in great wreaths around Akayna's head and body. From another pouch he took holy corn pollen and scattered it around Akayna and all over her body as a sign of fruitfulness and productivity.

As Akayna stood motionless, the shaman planted four prayer sticks on the ground. Each pointed to the four corners of the earth. The feathers of the prayer sticks would move with the slightest air to send supplications to the four winds. All during the procedure, the shaman kept singing to show that singing was the life's breath that consecrated all the parts of the ritual. Faint and emotional, Akayna dared not falter or show weakness, but willed herself to remain steady until the conclusion of the ceremony.

Suddenly, the medicine man stopped singing. He stood on the opposite side of the fire, faced Akayna, and with both hands lifted skyward, raised his voice in a piercing shriek. A responding shriek came from the assembled crowd outside.

The shaman peeled back the skin covering the lodge opening and stepped back. Akayna stepped forward to be greeted by the crowd. Cheers, calls, hand clapping and the throbs of multiple drums greeted her as she stood before them — their squaw sachem.

Dancing and feasting began almost immediately.

The tribe had been through many deprived moments with the war and the loss of their leader. They had left their homes for this temporary camp outside the swamp, and they were worried about the future English encroachment on their lands, but tonight they would put their problems out of their minds.

Fires glowed around a semicircle in the center of the field. Cooking had been going on all day, and the smell of succulent meats roasting over the many fires was tantalizing to Akayna. Still, she had to wait until the presentation of gifts before she could eat. She sat on a small, overturned log as gifts of wampum, bowls, animal skins, knives and other trinkets were piled high on the log on both sides of her. Her warrior troops presented themselves with a thunderous dance. Their moccasins stirred the dust of the earth, as the bells around their ankles pealed and clattered with joy as the men danced and jumped, one higher than the other, for her approval. The dancing lasted almost an hour and then, exhausted, the men ceased and the food was served at last.

Huge platters, serving boards of grilled *aquaunduut,* which was bluefish, *monasquisse'etash* and *askutasq,* which was corn and beans, simmered with bits of meat were served in steaming bowls. There were servings of grilled *mohtukquas* or rabbit, a turtle soup, roasted venison and bear meat steaks. There was plenty for all.

Akayna had already fasted for three days, and even though she was ravenously hungry, her nerves and her stomach would accept nothing more than a little soup and a fragment of johnnycake.

Tomorrow, she thought, *I start a new life.* Her duties would be to call the people together for meetings and ceremonies, to keep the tribal roll of names, to provide leadership and inspiration, and if need be, to declare war. The Council of Mothers and the Council of Elders, a caucus, would advise her, but decisions would be hers to make in the end.

As she looked out over the people who had depended on her father and now were looking to her for guidance, she thought of Ibraha. She wished that he were with her. *I need you, Ibraha. Where are you?* The depth of her loneliness was overwhelming when she slept alone that night in the new *wetu* assigned to her, squaw sachem.

CHAPTER TWENTY

Dressed in a lightweight wool burnoose, a blue cotton turban on his head, Ibraha expected to attract some attention when he walked into the Cape Cod village of Monset. He recalled Khamseen's distasteful experience of being taken for an escaped slave. In his native clothing, he hoped to be seen differently.

Homesick English settlers had tried to capture a replica of the small seaside villages they had left behind in England. The town of Monset was typically such a place with thatched roofs, small multiflowered gardens, trellises, and gates with flagstone paths leading to the tiny front doors. There was even an attempt at a small village green in the town's center.

Ibraha recognized the same fall colors in the brilliant yellow chrysanthemums, purple asters and cheerful marigolds that he remembered studded the white walls in his country, Spain. The sight inflicted momentary pangs of regret that he might never see Torremolinos again. But for now he knew he'd do better to focus his thoughts and energies on his goal to find and claim his love, Akayna.

As he walked around the small green, he tried to

figure out a plan to help him in his search. This was a new, untamed country. He had already heard from the Indians about how land-hungry the English were, but surely they were in need of persons with skills, no matter what color that person might be. He would be sure to present himself in that manner, and if there were new skills to be learned, he'd do that, too.

Ibraha was not too proud to say "teach me." All of his life he had been eager to learn new skills, meet and try to understand new people, taste a variety of foods — he made himself comfortable wherever he found himself. It would be no different here in this new country. Even his name, Ibraha, that his mother gave him when he was born was from the old Hebrew, Abraham, which she told her son meant "father to the many."

He decided that perhaps it might be best if he did not reveal his knowledge of English and try to get by with limited Spanish and maybe pidgin English. That is, until he could decide his course. Less would be expected of him.

"Ho' there, ye wearin' the frock!"

Ibraha turned at the sound. A grizzled-looking fisherman pointed at Ibraha with a stubby corn pipe. He moved over on the fallen log on which he sat to make room for Ibraha. "An' ye be?" the man asked, as he gestured at Ibraha with his pipe.

"Me illamo Ibraha," Ibraha said in Spanish, as he pointed to his own chest.

"Ibraha.. Wal, Ibraha, ye came on the *Sea Treasure*, eh? Gone now, eh? Sailed without ye!" The fisherman's right eye squinted from the pipe's smoke.

"*Sea Treasure*," Ibraha said in an accented voice,

shrugged his shoulders and made a sign of dismissal with his hands to indicate that indeed the ship had left him behind.

"Wal, yer big 'n' strong 'n' healthy and truly a black man at that, ain't ye? Seen yer type fellas down Cape of Good Hope when I sailed the seas in me younger years."

Ibraha merely smiled. He would be patient. So far he had sensed no hostility from the man, only apparent curiosity. They sat quietly. The fisherman puffed on his pipe and Ibraha observed the activity in the village square. Several small children played in the area and housewives greeted and chatted with each other as they went about their errands and daily chores.

"Boats, ships, ye know 'bout them?" the man asked Ibraha. He picked up a stick from the ground and traced in the dirt an outline of a boat with sail.

"Boat, ship," he pointed at the tracing.

"Ah, boat, ship," Ibraha parroted and he nodded eagerly. "Boat, ship," he pantomimed waves in the sea.

"Ah'd say ye've come 'round at the right time. Bin lookin' fer someone to help caulk me boat. Know ennythin' 'bout whales?"

"Whales?" Ibraha's heart leaped, but he feigned puzzlement. He had been on many whale hunts as a young man in the Bay of Biscay with the Basque in northern Spain. "Whales?" he repeated.

The fisherman picked up the stick again and this time sketched in the dirt a picture of a giant fish.

"Si, aha! Whale!" Ibraha bobbed his head up and down in acknowledgment.

A wide grin broke over the man's face as he pointed with his stubby pipe to himself and back to Ibraha.

"Whales," he said. "Oil, blubber... money, you, me."

Ibraha understood exactly what the man meant. Someone to help him repair his boat, someone to help him hunt whales in the waters of Cape Cod.

Using gestures and pantomime, a deal was struck between Ibraha and the old salt, who said his name was Alan Rosewood.

"Cose ye wouldn' hev' no way o' knowin', but the darn separatin' ones, the folks o' religious beliefs, they're agin me fishin' fer whales. Want me ter spen' me time listenin' ter their preachin' 'n' teachin' 'n' farmin', but 'tis a good livin' ah'm after. Got a wife back in England waitin' fer me."

Ibraha listened intently, pretending little or no understanding, but he realized that this man was not a Puritan, but a simple English commoner seeking a way to improve his lot in life.

Rosewood stood up and beckoned for Ibraha to follow him. "Let me show somethin' to yer."

They left the village green and walked about a mile out of the small town toward the beach. They continued down the beach for another mile. On the shore, a bedraggled cutter lay bobbing at anchor. The single masted fore and aft rigged sailing vessel with a running bowsprit was in need of much overhauling. Ibraha could see from where he stood on the beach that most of the cedar planks in the hull of the ship needed to be recaulked.

"Ah kno' she looks some bad, but she's in pretty fair shape, 'cept fer them seams that need tendin' to. Look," he pointed to the name painted on the transom of the boat, *Mighty Maiden.* That's fer me missus, one o' the stronges' wimmin ah know!"

He grinned sheepishly at Ibraha, who responded with a smile. He was beginning to feel optimistic and hopeful about his future. He knew how to caulk a boat; had done the job many times before. If only he had his oak hammer and wedging iron, and perhaps a makeshift caulking hook, he could pull out the old putty and cotton where it was no longer tight and replace the old material with new. He'd have the *Mighty Maiden* watertight in no time. It would be good to have some busy work to do while he sought information about Akayna and her tribe.

A large animal bounded toward them from the deck of the ship and ran over the beach to Alan Rosewood, who greeted the dog with rough caresses. "'Tis me pal, Jocko, Ibraha, cum all the way over from England on the ship wid me! A good shipmate 'e was, too!" The dog bounded about the two men, its tawny-colored coat healthy and shiny. It seemed eager and excited to see its master again.

"Jes' let 'im 'ave a smell o' yer 'n' pet 'im gently," Rosewood demonstrated to Ibraha. "'E'll be the bes' frien' ye'll ever 'ave. Naught will bother ye if 'es aroun'. Them separatists," he spat on the sand, "didn' like the idear o' me bringin' 'im to the new world, but ah paid 'is passage so naught could say no."

Ibraha stood quite still while the dog sniffed around him. Apparently satisfied that this person had been accepted by his master, the dog wagged his shaggy tail enthusiastically when Ibraha gave him a gentle pat on the head.

Rosewood said, "Ye can live on board the *Mighty Maiden* if that would suit ye."

So with Jocko at his side, Ibraha made himself quite

comfortable on the ship. Once each day, Allan Rosewood brought food that the two men would share as they worked.

Ibraha made a mallet out of a piece of oak he found in the woods near the beach. He made a makeshift caulking hook out of an old piece of iron he found on the ship. For the deep seams of the old ship he used old rope fiber that he rolled in pine tar and formed the strand so that he could wedge it into the plank spaces. For lesser spaces Ibraha used long strips of cotton tucked carefully into the seams. After that, he covered each new seam with a stiff, putty-like compound.

Alan Rosewood was pleased. "Ah, lad, ye know what yer doin' ah must say." He admired Ibraha's bulging, gleaming shoulders and arm muscles as the African hit with solid, true motions, and with the hammer and wedge tucked and tightened the loops of cotton and hemp. "Got a regular rhythm to yer work! The *Mighty Maiden's* goin' to be fit fer a king, 'specially after she gits a new coat o' paint!"

Ibraha grunted as he kept to his task. He hit the hammer against the iron wedge, the sound satisfying to his ears, but his mind was elsewhere.

As he swung his oak hammer, he wondered if Akayna was safe. What had happened to the tribe with its leader dead?

Ibraha was glad that no one recognized him. Even though Rosewood knew he had been aboard the *Sea Treasure*, he was not going to lose his assistant, so he suggested that Ibraha make himself scarce when anyone came near the boat. Most feared Jocko, anyway.

Often at night, as he lay on the open deck, with Jocko at his feet, Ibraha tracked the stars as they moved through the night. Their brilliance reminded him of the star shine of Akayna's eyes. The black velvet night sky's softness touched his soul with a sweet remembrance of Akayna's delicate lips on his. He ached for her presence. Somewhere the same stars shone for her, the same moonglow bathed her lovely face. She must be close by. He listened to the whispering breath of the wind in the tall, straight, dark-green pine trees. He wished he could scale their heights and fly in great bursts of speed to wherever she was that very night. The murmur of the ocean waves as they struck the sandy shore, struggling for a futile purchase of land only to slip away back to the vast ocean, finally lulled him to sleep with Akayna's name on his lips. She was his first thought of the morning and his last whisper before sleep. He could not wait much longer to start his search.

It came sooner than he had hoped. Alan Rosewood needed "dead eyes" for the shrouds of the sails, needed new sailcloth and more riggings. Some of the goods, he told Ibraha, should have come into Boston on the latest packet from England. So he had taken the Plymouth-Taunton coach to Boston.

"Should be back tomorry evenin'," he told Ibraha. "Jocko'll be yer company. Naught will pester ye if 'es 'round."

That first night Ibraha felt compelled to go into the woods. He was anxious and restless. Could he find any clues? Any traces of the missing tribe? He left Jocko on board the *Mighty Maiden* and started across the sandy beach before entering the woods.

He was not aware of it, but someone was trailing him. Earlier, an Indian lad of about fourteen, curious about the English, had returned to the former campsite.

He wandered to the shoreline at dusk, where he saw the African who worked with the Yengee on the boat.

He remembered that the sachem's daughter had returned from her long voyage accompanied by two black men. Now the *Sea Treasure* had left, but one man remained. What did it mean? Should he tell the new squaw sachem? He decided instead to tell the Keeper-of-the-Faith.

CHAPTER TWENTY-ONE

In her new role as designated leader of her people, Akayna felt an almost physical wrench in her heart between her duty to the tribe and her deep, ever-hollow yearning for her lover, Ibraha. *I cannot face my life without him,* she sighed to herself. *I need his strength, his encouragement, his love. Will I ever relive the sweet moments I knew with him on the Sea Treasure? Oh, Kautantowwit,* she prayed, *God of the south winds, the good, kind winds of love, please return my love, my other self! I ache so for him.*

She would have prayed even harder had she known what malevolence lay in Khamseen's heart. She had not reckoned with him.

When he had left the harbor on the next high tide, Khamseen's intention was to remove himself as quickly as possible from the madness of the colonists. They dared look on him as a slave! He, who had built and sailed a ship across the Atlantic the same as they. And the Indians, well, their habits and customs were far less developed than those he had learned as a pampered child in Torremolinos.

His bitterness extended as well to Ibraha, who, with

his treachery, as he saw it, had snared the Indian girl. She should be his! For Khamseen, the past months of struggling with difficult celibacy hardened his anger. At the same time, his loins quivered at the memory of the lovely girl. Would all of his sacrifices be for nothing?

He had set the compass and his sails to move out of the Cape waters, travel close to inland until he reached the Elizabeth Islands, then move toward Montauk Point off the tip of Long Island. But after the vessel had moved confidently over the blue-green waters and was making excellent progress, he changed his mind.

"When we reach Martha's Vineyard," he told Aftar, his wheelman, "change course and tack to the east. I want to go to Boston."

"Aye, sir," the pilot answered. "That means we will move around the elbow of the Cape, out into the deeper waters after Provincetown."

Although anxious to head south, back to Spain and the North African coast, Aftar saw the determination in Khamseen's raven-black eyes. He dared not dispute the man. Instead, he kept his counsel and pulled forward in his mind that since Khamseen had gotten them to this wild place, surely, God in all heavens, he could see them safely home.

"When we reach Boston, we'll anchor in the harbor. I plan to take Zaid and Omar with me to get the supplies we will need for our voyage home."

"Will you get new spokes for the wheel, Captain?" Aftar pointed to the missing spokes ripped out during the storm.

"Aye, we could have bad weather before we get too far along. We probably should not wait until we reach

Virginia or the Carolinas for the provisions and replacements we need for the ship. But, I must see this city of Boston," he told Aftar as he looked out over the dancing waves. "I have heard from Englishmen that it was built on marshland, with a deep harbor facing the city."

"So I have heard, Captain," Aftar agreed. "But be alert. There are many scoundrels and opportunists about. They may see you as an escaped slave."

"If I wear my turban and burnoose, they will know I am a foreigner."

• • •

Alan Rosewood took special notice of the tall black man who entered Bascomb's boat yard. He could see that the man's coloring was much like Ibraha's. Indeed, the clothing was similar. The heavy striped burnoose that Khamseen wore made him stand out in vivid contrast to the sober homespun clothing worn by the Puritans. Beneath the burnoose, Rosewood saw Khamseen's blue cotton trousers, tied at the ankles, and a light tan, soft woolen shirt that only accented the deep, dusky hue of his skin. His shoes were his best; tooled leather turned up at the toes, in the eastern manner. A turban of blue cotton was twisted into a simple covering for his head. His was a presence not to be denied.

Ned Bascomb stared at the black man who looked like someone from Arabian nights. The wonder of it all showed in his faded blue eyes. There was a hoarse crackle in Ned's throat when he spoke.

"Yes?" he had to clear his throat before the word came out clearly. "Yes?" he tried again.

He almost jumped when Khamseen responded in a clear voice in English with an accent that Bascomb could not quite place.

"You have ship's supplies for sale?" Khamseen inquired.

"Aye, some. 'N wot be yer needs?" Bascomb asked, never taking his eyes from the stranger's face.

Khamseen, too, held Bascomb's face locked with his own direct eye contact as he ticked off the items he wanted with his fingers. "Sailcloth, rope, halyards, a jib and anchor. Turned spokes for my wheel if you have the same."

Bascomb's eyes narrowed as he considered the scope of the African's list. This purchase would come to a pretty penny. "Accept nought but hard coin for payment," he blustered as he gave a sidelong glance in Rosewood's direction. He knew Rosewood was listening, and, indeed, he was glad to have a witness if anything should go wrong.

As an old retired seaman, Ned Bascomb had seen Africans, Chinese, East Indians, Berbers, and the like, men of many races in his travels, but he recognized the rarity of such a man as the one standing before him in New England. But, then, Boston was a port city and people were bound to come from many parts of the world.

Khamseen was observant as well, and he had taken notice of the disbelief in the merchant's voice and the disdain that such a one as he could stand before the shopkeeper and seek supplies for a ship.

"I have what is needed for my purchases," Khamseen stated, and in a movement so quick it seemed like a magician's trick, he produced several British florins.

Bascomb's face flushed with grudging compliance as he scuttled about the dingy boat shop gathering the items Khamseen wanted.

"Ye'll be needin' 'elp to get these stores to yer ship?" he questioned.

"Nay, will pay now. My men will be here before day's end to take them aboard the *Sea Treasure*."

Sea Treasure! Alan Rosewood's ears pricked forward as he heard the words. That was the ship that had stranded Ibraha in Monset village. And if this African spoke English, no doubt Ibraha could, too. Why had he pretended not to know the language? He wondered what it all meant. He needed Ibraha for his whale hunt. He was determined to get enough money from this one last adventure so he could return home and retire.

• • •

Khamseen made more purchases that day. Staples such as beans, rice, some salt meat, vegetables like potatoes and turnips, baskets of apples, and casks of fresh water. No wine was available from the abstaining Puritans. His last stop was at the village chemist who fashioned elixirs, potions and ground herbs for the ill when they had suffered enough to ask for help.

"Arsenic, you say?" the wizened, sallow-faced clerk questioned.

"Aye, many, many rats aboard my ship," Khamseen repeated. "Many rats."

Khamseen's pride was again getting the best of him. From the time he was a boy, he was determined to have his way. No matter how hard his father, Mustepha, had tried, he had never been able to tame the selfish streak he saw in his son. He realized that after Khamseen's mother died, he had spoiled him.

Khamseen grew to manhood and with his size, good looks and quick mind, he became accustomed to believing whatever he wanted he would have. His impulsive behavior often put him in danger, but he was clever enough to escape what would have been disastrous to a lesser man.

Khamseen still wanted Akayna; now, with Ibraha in the picture, the challenge to gain her affection was more burning than ever. A picture of Ibraha and Akayna rose in his mind. He would return to that place on the Cape and somehow find the pair that were causing such tormenting hatred to rise like gorge in his throat.

• • •

Ned Bascomb had joined Alan Rosewood as he stood at the window and watched the departing African. He put the question to Rosewood, "Wal. Wot do ye mek o' that?"

"Dunno, 'cept I believe 'es first mate is right now on me boat, the *Mighty Maiden.* 'E," nodded Alan in Khamseen's direction, "was s'posed to hev' left these parts a week or so ago."

"By now, then," muttered Bascomb, "should be on the 'igh seas."

"Wonder why 'e come all the way to Boston fer supplies. 'Tis out o' the way, to come 'ere, when he could hev' passed Nantucket, Long Island, all places along the way for such like. Methinks 'es up to somethin'."

"Talbot!" Bascomb bellowed to his helper, a lad that hurried to him from a back room. "Run out 'n' keep an eye on the black feller that jes' left here. Mind 'e don' see yer followin' 'im!"

"Sir!" The young man tipped his cap and was gone.

When he reported back several hours later, Rosewood had made it his business to be there to get information firsthand. Not only did he hear about the visit to the chemist's shop, but he was informed that Talbot had seen Khamseen leave Mistress Penniman's dress cottage. The African had bought woman's things, Talbot said; dresses, yards of silk and linen, ribbons, laces, almost everything Mistress Penniman had in stock, she told Talbot.

Rosewood slapped his hand down on Bascomb's counter with such force that jars of lead pencils, boxes of bolts and nuts, sprang free from the dusty surface. "By God, that's it! I knew it! There's allus a woman in the picture. I'd 'eard the story before, but put little stock in it."

"What story?" Bascomb wanted to know.

"Why, about two African men who jes' come into these parts, bringin' back the chief sachem's daughter."

"Back from where?"

"Oh, the chief paid Henry Kendall much wampum ter whisk 'er off to safety, but the scoundrel sells 'er off ter some bloke in Spain. Niver did trust 'im. So that's why," mused Rosewood, "Ibraha's been so quiet. The chief died 'n' the rest o' the tribe disappeared. The girl, too. Now I know why my frien' 'as ben listenin' 'n' watchin'. Wants to fin' the girl."

"'N' if yer right, seems as if this other one does, too."

• • •

Alan Rosewood returned to Bascomb's boat yard for the third time that day. He wanted to find out if Khamseen had picked up his purchases. Bascomb met him at the doorway with a shrug of his shoulders and upraised open palms, a sign of conclusion.

"Gone, a'ready?" Rosewood asked.

"Aye, took early delivery and was leavin' on the four o' clock tide. In a 'urry, seems like. 'E'd made up 'is mind to move along."

"Mus' do the same," Rosewood said. "Dunno wot it means for Ibraha 'n' me, but got ter mek sure nothin' stands betwixt me 'n' that whale hunt. Need Ibraha fer that. No other harpooner in these parts that I know of that would be of use ter me."

Like any entrepreneur whose financial plans were threatened, he couldn't wait until the next noon when the Plymouth-Taunton coach left for Monset. Instead, he secured a mare that could be tied to the back of the coach on its return trip to Boston. He left his father's stickpin as a guarantee of that. It was the only piece of valuable jewelry he had, but he knew he'd get it back.

With luck, Alan Rosewood thought, he could make the trip about as quickly as the ship could sail around the elbow and into the harbor of the Wampanoags. He'd have to tell his friend, Ibraha, that Khamseen had not sailed.

The young mare was accommodating and strong, so he made the trip in less time than he thought possible. He didn't push the horse; he stopped at Pembroke, Plymouth, and Sandwich for water and brief rests. He reached the *Mighty Maiden* late that night, the "moon cusser's" night. A night that robbers and thieves would curse the moon for shining so brightly they could not lure unwary ships to their sandy beaches to steal from the foundering vessels.

The *Mighty Maiden* lay peaceful and serene. Rosewood loved the ship, and she looked even more beautiful to him now that she had been caulked, painted and made seaworthy. He heard Jocko's growl as he placed his foot on the first step of the gangplank. "Easy, lad, 'tis me." He ruffled the fur on the dog's great head as he saw Ibraha move from his sleeping place on the shadowed deck.

"Aye, Ibraha, glad yer up. Lots to tell yer. First off, I know yer speaks the king's English..." He watched as Ibraha's eyebrows rose in surprise. "Yep, met yer Captain in Boston."

"Khamseen! In Boston?"

"If that's 'is name, 'twas 'im. Now, not askin' why yer didn' let on ye knew the language; had yer reasons, I guess. Thought ye'd be seen as a runaway?"

Again he saw agreement in Ibraha's eyes as he nodded his head. "Hummm, figgered as much. Wal, ye've been straight wi' me. I believe yer means to 'elp me wi' me whale hunt, but the lass, that's the problem. Eh?"

They sat, each one on a pile of coiled ropes, each engrossed in thoughts of what lay ahead.

Ibraha spoke first. "I must find Akayna. I know now that Khamseen will be looking for her. But I love her and I know she loves me. Khamseen was sorely disappointed that he could not engage in trade here, that your English thought him to be a slave. Not an easy man; wants what he wants. Besides, he has a threat on his head. Still has to return the emir's ship."

"Emir?" Rosewood looked confused, then apparently light dawned on him as he warned Ibraha. "I saw two men dressed in clothes like ye wear sometimes, hangin' 'round near the Tea Harbor. Mus' be the emir's!"

"By all that's holy, I've got to warn Khamseen!"

"Nay, frien' don't expect 'im till the mornin' tide. I'll go 'n' speak ter 'im. Then we'll see if we kin get news o' the lass yer seekin'. Rough tho' I may be, know whot it is ter love a good woman."

"About my English," Ibraha offered, "learned from sailors about the city and the many ports when whaling with my uncle."

"But ye were afeard?"

"Been a free man all my life, with seaman's papers too. Intend to be free in this new country as well." Ibraha's voice was strong with determination.

Rosewood nodded his head in agreement and admiration for the friend who had come into his life.

• • •

Khamseen had not seen the emir's agents who lurked on Boston's muddy street that day. His single-mindedness had made him unwary. When he met Zaid and Omar at the loading dock, the two young men piled the yards of sailcloth, coils of rope, halyards, and the other items in the dinghy. Khamseen was anxious to get back to the anchored *Sea Treasure* so he could begin to carry out his plan to deal with Ibraha and Akayna. As the dinghy moved across the water toward the ship, Khamseen's thoughts were concentrated on the beautiful Indian girl that was rightfully his.

When the dinghy finally reached the *Sea Treasure,* he climbed up the ladder and hoisted himself over the ship's rail. Not until he was aboard, did he become aware of the ominous silence that greeted him. Why was there no one at the wheel? As he looked more closely, he saw draped over the wheel a flag with a green five-pointed star, the seal of Solomon outlined in black at the center of a red field. It barely moved back and forth. Khamseen's heart nearly stopped at the sight of the cloth.

He turned to escape, to warn Zaid and Omar as they clambered up the ladder behind him, but it was too late.

"Thief! No one steals from the emir!" Khamseen heard, as two swarthy-skinned men dressed in dark brown burnooses reached for him.

His destiny had found him.

CHAPTER TWENTY-TWO

Voices came from every corner of the ceremonial lodge. Akayna's ears were stunned by the strident cries hurled at her. It felt like a bombardment of arrows.

"The Yengees have taken our crops! Stolen our food! Our fishing and hunting grounds are not ours any longer! They have even put wooden houses where our *wetus* were!"

Each native was pleading his cause, and tempers were rising. There was talk of war.

Akayna, dressed in a simple white deerskin shift, wore a wreath crown of feathers on her head. Her wampum belt that had belonged to her father was draped across her chest. It was one of her decorations of authority. She motioned to the Keeper-of-the-Faith, and he pushed a small stool toward her. She stood on it and raised her hand for silence. Respectfully, there was immediate quiet.

Inwardly, Akayna quivered with nerves, but she knew the survival of her people depended on her next move. She chose her words carefully, her voice was low and controlled. "My brave warriors. I hear the pain and anger in your hearts. I know of your impatience. I, too, feel your wrath toward the Yengees. We have been used and our friendship betrayed. We followed the wisdom and guidance of the Great Spirit, *Kautantowwit,* the wisdom we have followed for millions of sunrisings, and we shared our food, our knowledge, with the ones who came to our shores. We helped them live, and in return they have given us nothing. They brought instead death from their diseases and death from their drink and their guns. Still, they want more! They want our land."

Grunts, groans and stamps of approval from the assembled warriors let Akayna know that both she and the group shared the same assessment of the situation. She continued.

"The loss of our homes and land is very great, but we are alive. The Wampanoag still live. We are together as one people. Should we leave this place for another or should we stay here and fight? We have already suffered a heavy loss," she referred to her father, "and although we try to be of good cheer, *Kutchimmoke,* the loss is still felt."

Akayna stopped speaking for a moment to allow her words to have an affect on her listeners. The room was very warm; the men's bodies glistened with perspiration mixed with the bear grease that had been applied to keep insects from their naked skin. Slowly, Akayna continued.

"The Council of Revered Mothers has already met to discuss this problem. Their solution is to 'find new fields, move to a safer place.' The Council of Elder Men has met also and they say, 'War with the Yengees so we can return to our homeland.' The caucus is divided."

Immediately on hearing those words, some of the younger men began to react. They shouted, raised their fists and bellowed with the familiar war whoops and cries for battle.

Akayna stopped the dissent with an upraised palm. "I have sworn to keep our tribe together, whatever the decision may be. We already know the Yengees have many guns. We could request the help of our brothers, the Nausets, at the far side of the Cape, or perhaps the Narragansetts from the Providence Plantations of Rhode Island, or there is still another way. We could seek peace with the Yengees. I propose a meeting with both councils and a decision will be made soon."

The meeting was over and Akayna returned to her *wetu*. The loneliness and burgeoning anxiety she felt weighed heavily on her. She knew the English wanted to annihilate the tribe, they were so land-hungry. Mother Earth meant for the land to be used wisely by her children, Akayna believed, not owned by a few. She sighed as she sat alone on a log stool. She did not want to ask another tribe for help in fighting the enemy. Her father had never done so, and she could not bear the thought of such an action as her first major decision as the new squaw sachem.

Later that same day, she met with both councils and offered her idea of a peace treaty. The Council of Elder Men and the Council of Revered Mothers discussed the problem. The men wanted war, but the women prevailed. They insisted peace should be attempted first, before war. "What good will it do for us to send the flowers of our family, our young men, to war, to return, perhaps, maimed or killed? We could then lose our nation twice, without the seed for another generation."

When Akayna told the Keeper-of-the-Faith about her plan for a treaty, he agreed to help her write it and he promised to take it to the king's magistrate in Monset. The shaman was more than the medicine man of the tribe; as Keeper-of-the-Faith, he held the responsibility of interceding, of using techniques and rituals that would help the tribe over stormy paths.

He understood the unhappiness, the heavy grief that burdened Akayna. From her great-aunt, he had learned about Akayna's feelings and concerns; her attitude toward her duties and responsibilities. Her great-aunt had also discussed with him the conversation about Akayna's perceived debt to Khamseen. She told the shaman that Akayna truly loved Ibraha, who had disappeared after Anesquam's death.

He agreed with the old woman that Akayna had certainly satisfied any debt she may have owed Khamseen when she saved his ship.

"And you, revered mother, you realize as your squaw sachem she may marry anyone of her own choosing."

"But the one she wants is not here," the old woman said. "The ship has sailed."

He reassured the old woman. "I will help our squaw sachem. I will appeal to the kindly spirits and pay homage to them in her behalf." He patted the beaded bag that he carried around his waist, as if to be certain his amulets and herbs for his potions were in place.

He understood Akayna's state of mind. Part priest, part elder statesman, the shaman had noticed the sadness and trouble reflected in the young girl's face. Her burden of responsibility seemed to weigh her down physically. In only a short time her happiness of being returned to her home and loved ones had been changed to an unexpected burden. He knew she was aware of her unique responsibilities. He had seen her sick and heaving one morning behind her *wetu*.

There was something very sad about the way life had pushed Akayna first into one dark crevice and then another. As a child, when her mother had been snatched from her by a white hunter's poor aim, she had been forced to face harsh reality. Happiness seemed to have passed her by. The Keeper-of-the-Faith vowed to help her. He would use the most potent magic he knew.

He found her later that day in the center of the village. With the other women, she was pounding corn to make cornmeal. The mill was a large flat rock, almost like a table. There were several women standing with her, grinding their corn by rolling round stones over the coarse grain. It was understandable that Akayna would seek solace and comfort from the other women. She might be the squaw sachem, but she was a woman, and it was important to her that she not separate herself from her peers. The stories they told and the songs they shared as they worked lifted Akayna's spirits. Again, she felt deep pride in being one of the Children of the First Light. Surely, she thought, only good could come to them as followers of the First Light, the sun.

Sometime later the Keeper sat with Akayna in her *wetu*. A small fire of very hot stones burned in the center of the room. On the stones the Keeper-of-the-Faith had placed several slender pointed sticks. These were to be charred on the ends so that picture art could be drawn on the birch bark to be used for the treaty. "I have fresh, clean white birch bark for a treaty," he told her.

"Good, my Keeper-of-the-Faith. I shall dictate the terms both councils have decided on, and with which I agree."

The shaman grunted, spread out a large roll of the inner side of the birch bark. He drew the word pictures with a flourish as Akayna outlined the councils' wishes.

"First, the councils insist no more land is to be sold to the Englishmen. Second, we must be allowed to continue to use our hunting and fishing grounds without interference. Third, no more *beson* is to be sold to our people. Fourth, we must be allowed to return to our homes by the ocean whenever we wish, without restrictions. In return for this, we will share food and teach skills necessary for this life to the Yengees."

• • •

Governor General George Sheridan was interrupted at his afternoon tea when he was informed by his aide that an Indian requested to see him.

"What does he want?" the governor sputtered, angry at being bothered at what he called "the only really civil thing in this wild place," his afternoon tea.

"He says, sir, that he brings a treaty."

"What does a savage know of treaties. Where is he from?"

"I asked him, sir, and he says that it is from the squaw sachem of the Wampanoag tribe of the Algonquin nation, whoever that is," the aide muttered.

Governor Sheridan had deep feelings and he was essentially a man of peace. All he wanted was to serve the king as well as he could and return to England to live out the rest of his life with his wife in a small English village. What did this intruder mean in his life? More problems, he was sure.

He sighed, replaced his teacup in its saucer on a side table. "Send the savage in, but remain close by," he told his aide.

Governor General Sheridan was a small man, barely five-feet-five-inches tall. Despite his intentions to the contrary, his weight was a constant problem to him. He loved food, good wine and a sedentary life. His florid complexion and tiny dark eyes in his quite round face made him look deceptively like a merry elf. He wore a black suit with a red brocade vest, and brass buttons which marched over his rotund belly seemed to make a caricature of him. He was bald as well. The scant fringes of hair he combed forward added to his puckish look. A less imposing person for authority could scarcely be found.

When the Keeper-of-the-Faith came through the door, the contrast between the two men was quite noticeable. Sheridan was short and stocky, clothed in heavy garb, whereas the shaman was tall and sinewy. There were slashes of white paint on his forehead, the symbol of his rank as a medicine man. He wore a breechcloth of otter skin. It was about a yard and a half long and was suspended from a belt made of soft doeskin. The flaps hung down front and back. He wore a mantle made of woven hemp that extended to his thighs. It swung from his left shoulder so that his right arm was free. A border design in red, blue and yellow decorated the hem edge. On his head he wore a leather band with three large turkey feathers fastened to stand upright in the front. His leggings were long tubes of deerskin, and his moccasins were of soft smoke-tanned buckskin. In his right hand the Keeper-of-the-Faith carried his peace pipe, and under his left arm he carried a rolled deerskin containing the birch bark treaty. His long black hair fell to his shoulders and his jet-black eyes were straightforward and piercing. His skin coloring was that of a sun-bronzed god. He made an impressive figure. The governor's office seemed too small for him.

Governor Sheridan had stood when the shaman entered the room, but he was so startled when the Indian began to speak English in a formal, oratorical manner, that he sat down quickly behind his desk.

In English, learned from Sachem Anesquam, the shaman explained his mission. He unrolled the deerskin with its birch bark scroll and pointed to each picture as he explained the meaning of each. He concluded by pointing attention to Akayna's signature. "She is our squaw sachem," the shaman stated. "Our fathers and mothers appointed her as the tribe's leader after the death of her father, our chief sachem." He added solemnly, "Her name means Peaceful One in our language."

"I see, but she is a squaw. You mean I'm to sign a treaty with a woman? Unheard of..." he said.

"If you wish peace, you will sign," the Keeper-of-the-Faith explained stoically. "She is our true and present leader. We have no other." He made direct eye contact with the unsettled Englishman and then he spoke abruptly. "I wait." He sat down cross-legged on the floor directly in front of the governor's desk.

This behavior was unexpected by the Englishman. His appointment and his instructions from the king had not included negotiating with the red-skinned savages. Mainly, as he saw it, his duties were to see that the king's laws were obeyed and that all revenues due the king were collected and sent back to London.

The shaman recognized the unease of his opponent, but his concern was to complete his mission and he was determined not to return to Akayna without doing so. He sat as immovable as a stone. Governor Sheridan was perplexed with the change in the Indian's demeanor. It was almost as if he had left his body and transported himself to another place. The whole scene upset the governor. He could see he would not easily remove the Indian from his office. The town council that met to discuss town affairs would not be meeting for another month. Even if he chose, there was no method of getting them together from their farms and businesses to meet so he could get the stubborn Indian out of his office. For expediency's sake, Governor Sheridan, as the king's representative, would have to act.

With instructions to his aide, Sheridan left the room. "Watch him," he nodded toward the sitting shaman. He went into his small study to think. Such activity would have been impossible to do with that Indian staring into space.

To date, the major difficulties with the Indians had been the deaths of several soldiers and civilians at the hands of the Indians. Most of the settlers wanted to go after the Indians, but at the time, and even now, they were not sure where the tribe was located. Surely this shaman did not intend to lead them to his tribe. Never had he met a person with such control. Perhaps the military would insist that the Indian be detained, punished until he revealed the tribe's location. But Sheridan did not believe, from what he had just seen, the man would reveal anything. He would die first. And peace was really what he wanted. How else were the colonists to survive and prosper if there was no peace? As it was, the French from Canada were clamoring to seize some of the colonists' land. But that was another problem.

He stood and looked out of the mullioned window at the dusty streets of Monset. It was a far cry from the typical English village, but the sight of it brought an unexpected lump in the governor's throat. These people were trying so hard to create the familiar out of the raw, stark, unknown land of this wild place. He decided. If he signed this so-called "treaty" perhaps they would have a respite in which to try to form a little bit of England, of home, in this godforsaken place.

He returned to his office. "I will sign," he informed the shaman. "My aide will be my witness."

"I will be witness as well," the Keeper-of-the-Faith replied as he rose from the floor.

The Indian picked up the inkwell from the governor's desk, placed his thumb on the open end of the vial and stained his thumb with ink. Then he rolled his wet thumb on the birch bark. He took a quill and drew a stick figure. "My mark," he said gruffly.

The aide wrote his name, and then the governor put his signature below the shaman's mark. He poured sand over the damp spots and shook the sand onto the floor.

The shaman rolled the birch scroll up into the deer-skin covering and placed it under his left arm. He raised his right hand, palm outward, and spoke. "Peace," he said. He continued, "As long as the sun brings day, as long as the moon brings light, as long as the oceans kiss our shores — peace," he repeated, and he left the office, his business concluded.

CHAPTER TWENTY-THREE

The shaman left the town of Monset by way of the seashore. He felt in need of fresh air after his encounter in the English governor's small, stuffy room.

The tantalizing, invigorating sea air filled his lungs and seemed to purify his whole body. Why did the Yengees want to live in such small, dark places when Blessed Mother Earth opened her arms to give her children a soft, warm breast to lay on with fresh clean winds and the most brilliant blue skies for cover? He would never understand.

As he walked to the water's edge, he shaded his eyes with his hand and looked to his right. Nothing. He looked to his left and far in the distance he saw a dark shadow. Could be the boat the lad spoke about.

The shaman was aware that he might be followed by the Yengees. He had no intention of returning to the camp beyond the swamp until after dark. So he had time to investigate the young lad's findings.

He walked along the beach for almost two miles before he reached the cove where the *Mighty Maiden* was anchored. A deep roar greeted him as he neared the ship. He stood, immobile, as Jocko, the mastiff bounded toward him. The shaman spoke quietly to the animal. "Behave, little brother, I come as a friend."

The dog got down on his belly and crawled to the waiting Indian, indicating respect and obedience.

At the dog's bark, both Ibraha and Alan Rosewood looked over the deck railing, astonished at the animal's behavior.

"Niver would 'ave believed such a thing if ah 'adn't seen it wi' me own eyes," declared Alan. "An' ye be?" he spoke to the Keeper-of-the-Faith.

"Shaman, medicine man, Keeper-of-the-Faith of the Wampanoags," the Indian answered, but his eyes were riveted on the black man standing next to the Englishman. Was this the man who had captured the heart of his squaw sachem? It had to be. Silently, he thanked the Great Spirit for answering his prayer.

"Gor, ye speak the King's English!" Rosewood observed.

"Aye."

"But yer an' Indian!"

"That is so. I come for him," the shaman pointed at Ibraha.

"S'pose he chooses not to go?" Rosewood said.

"I go," Ibraha interjected quickly. If this man was one of Akayna's tribesmen, Ibraha would certainly go with him.

"Wal, be back soon, Ibraha. Got to get to sea soon 'n' start huntin' whales."

Ibraha nodded wordlessly. He had given the Englishman many days of hard labor in return for a place to rest until he could find his loved one. Would he see her soon?

The shaman sat on the beach and watched as the two

men continued their work on the boat. All day in the sun, back and forth, the thwack of hammers and the grinding of saws rang out as the boat began to take on a reasonable shape. It was dark before they stopped.

They built a fire on the sand and grilled freshly caught bluefish, roasted corn in the husks, and baked potatoes in the ashes. They drank a cool syllabub made of sassafras and milk. There was little conversation as they shared the food. Ibraha could hardly swallow his food, he was so anxious to be on the way. The evening moon had risen when finally the Indian stood and said, "Come," to Ibraha.

Ibraha stood, too, and turned to Alan Rosewood.

"Thank you for your help to me. I will get back for the whale hunt. I, Ibraha, promise." He extended his hand to the Englishman, who grasped it firmly.

"Come when ye can, lad," he said.

Ibraha nodded, picked up his blanket roll and followed the silent Keeper-of-the-Faith.

In all of his life, Ibraha had never seen such country. From the beach they walked into a woodland so dark and dense, it was hard to see paths or landmarks. At frequent intervals, the Indian stopped to make certain they were not being followed. He would look skyward to take his bearings from the stars.

Ibraha understood this because he had done the same many times at sea. Instead of ocean waves, they were traversing woods and swamps, but the feelings of jousting with the elements of nature were the same. Ibraha respected his guide for his obvious skill.

The Keeper had not mentioned Akayna, but Ibraha felt optimistic as he moved silently behind his guide. He had no premonition of disaster, no fear of harm, only an expectation of good will.

He and Akayna were no longer in danger of Khamseen's wrath. His efforts to warn Khamseen were too late, and he had learned from Rosewood of Khamseen's tragic end aboard the *Sea Treasure* at the hands of the emir's men. Ibraha bore the news with outward stoicism, but inwardly he grieved deeply for the man who had once been like a younger brother to him. With a heavy heart, he had vowed to send word to Mustepha.

Ibraha and the shaman stopped at the edge of the Great Swamp. The shaman pulled at some reeds on the shoreline and uncovered a small canoe with two oars in it. He gave one to Ibraha and took a seat in front of the African. Quietly they moved through the swampy waters. The mosquitoes and chiggers did not seem to bother the Indian; for his protection, Ibraha covered himself with his burnoose and wrapped a turban around his head. He received a little relief, but he would have endured even more if necessary. He knew, just knew, Akayna was close by. His heart hammered erratically in his chest. He thought the silent Keeper-of-the-Faith must surely hear it.

After an hour of stealthy movement in the swampy water, dodging hummocks and submerged tree roots, the canoe suddenly bumped into the grassy shoreline. The two men stepped onto boggy soil. They moved forward into a small copse of trees and shrubs.

"Wait here," the shaman told Ibraha. He disappeared from Ibraha's sight almost instantly.

Ibraha did as he was told. In the darkness he could see almost nothing. He waited.

• • •

Akayna lay on her bed of bearskin robes. She had been sleeping soundly in her *wetu* when the Keeper-of-the-Faith touched her hand lightly. She recognized the shaman instantly.

"Yes, Keeper. You have returned."

"The Yengees have signed the treaty. They have said 'yes' to peace."

"Now our people can live their lives as they always have. We thank you."

"May peace be with you in your life, squaw sachem, as well," the Keeper-of-the-Faith said as he backed out of the room.

As she watched the dignified man retreat from her presence, Akayna felt a hollow sense of relief. She was happy for her people, but would she ever have personal happiness?

She returned to her blanket of bearskins, the signed treaty resting on a stool nearby. She sighed restlessly and closed her eyes. Suddenly she felt as if there was someone else in the room. She opened her eyes and sat up, facing the flap of the *wetu*. Had the Keeper-of-the-Faith returned? The flap was pulled back slowly and a man stepped through.

Akayna gasped, stifling the scream that rose in her throat, both hands to her mouth as recognition took place. "Ibraha!" She ran into his arms as he stood in the doorway. "I thought I'd never see you again! Ibraha!"

Her words were lost in Ibraha's chest as his strong arms closed around her.

"I vowed I'd not leave until I found you, Akayna. Your Keeper-of-the-Faith found me and brought me to you."

"The Keeper? I don't understand."

"He said a lad had seen me, a black stranger in Monset, and he told the Keeper. Your Keeper-of-the-Faith is a wonderful man, Akayna. He knew I was looking for you."

"But why did you not return to your home with Khamseen?"

Akayna listened in silent amazement as Ibraha recounted what had happened from the time she last saw him. She frowned when he told her how Khamseen had met his fate.

"If you will have me, my future will be here with you, Akayna. Otherwise, I have no future. The promise of my living depends on the promise of my loving only you, my dearest Akayna. The Keeper-of-the-Faith has told me that you are the new squaw sachem, the leader of your people."

"Yes, when my..." she hesitated for a moment, "the sachem died, I was selected by both councils to be squaw sachem, Ibraha."

Ibraha still held her close, as if afraid of losing her again. He raised her chin toward his own face and looked directly into her dark eyes. "Akayna, will your people accept me? Now that you are squaw sachem, can I fit into your life?"

She took his hand and they walked to the pile of bearskins that formed her sleeping place. "As squaw sachem, I may marry anyone of my choosing."

He took both her hands in his. They were cold from apprehension. He kissed the palm of each one and placed them on his shoulders. He peered into her soft dark eyes and as he had done — it seemed like years ago — he gently released her dark cloud of hair. It fell around her golden-bronzed face as she sighed and tightened her arms around Ibraha's neck. She raised herself up on her toes, her bare feet between his booted ones as she strained to reach his mouth. He bent his head as his lips reached for hers, bruising her hungry lips with an intensity that surprised her. A slight moan escaped her as she felt Ibraha's strong tongue caressing her own tongue and lips.

Their bodies clung to each other as if they would melt into one another if possible. Ibraha stepped back and released the tie that held the loose, fine hemp sleeping shift that she wore. He held her arm as she stepped from the garment. Ibraha gasped when he saw the whole lean loveliness of her young body — her slender waist that curved into her rounded, soft hips; her beautiful, coltish legs. He had seen this woman-child change from a frightened waif exiled from her beloved homeland by schemers, scoundrels, yes, and even opportunists like Khamseen, to grow steadily into a woman of purpose and substance; to take on the duties of squaw sachem to her people. What was it about her that made him desire her so? Why did his loins ache so when he was near her or thought about her?

She was different. She was beautiful. But more than that, he felt, it was her dignity, her singleness of knowing herself, her inheritance of her Indian tradition and culture that made her who she was. Traveling from one hemisphere to the other had not robbed her of her identity as Akayna, a sachem's daughter. Ibraha's admiration for her personal being, along with her singular beauty, made him love this Indian woman.

Akayna saw the love in Ibraha's eyes as they reflected the light from the smoldering fire in the center of the room. She needed no words to know that this quiet giant of a man with the magnificent ebony body would protect, love and care for her for all of her life. She needed him and she wanted him.

At the moment, no words were needed between them. The bearskin felt soft and welcoming as Ibraha gently placed her on it. He leaned forward to kiss her eyes, her neck, the sweet hollow of her throat. His gentle but strong hand pursued the roundness of her breasts and her sensual response rewarded his efforts. He was delighted to be pleasing her. As she lay there on her back, the fall Hunter's moon shone through the smoke hole in the center of the *wetu*. It bestowed a heavenly benediction on the lovers, their dark and tawny skin tones merging together as their earthen-colored bodies fused into loving bliss. Akayna made short gasps as the tension mounted.

Ibraha touched her blue-black hair and rested his face in it as it spread over her shoulders. He caressed her face with his fingertips and felt the moist dampness of her skin. He waited for a moment until Akayna seemed more relaxed. Then shyly, she raised her arms to him in a welcoming gesture. He lowered himself to her. As the moment of fulfillment neared, Akayna's eyes grew wider and brighter until at last, in a shudder of passionate exhaustion, she recognized the soaring intimate ecstasy that she knew bound her to this man from across the sea — for the rest of her life.

"Akayna," Ibraha breathed, "at last, my love, at last." She replied in a voice so quiet he could hardly hear her.

"You are here, Ibraha. I love you."

CHAPTER TWENTY-FOUR

The two men sat face to face in the Keeper-of-the-Faith's small *wetu*.

"Many white men, as well as men from other tribes, have married our daughters. Of course, the English married in the building they call a church. But some did not. Because they accepted our daughters, they accepted our ways and so they married in our ceremonies."

"That is what I want, Keeper-of-the-Faith, to marry Akayna and become a turtle; a member of your clan." Strangely enough, Ibraha realized for the first time in a long time, he finally felt at home. He was at ease in the mat-covered *wetu*. It was not unlike some of the tented pavilions he had seen in Torremolinos, except those had been a bit more ventilated.

The shaman's *wetu* was quite closed, its walls made of willow branches covered with woven mats. Gourds, dried rattles from rattlesnakes, small bones of animals, pelts of otter, beaver and raccoon hung on the willow branches. Many carved figurines representing the Great Spirit swung from the domed roof like disembodied spirits. All around the crowded room, several pots with herbs, roots, various mixtures and potions offered a miasma of offensive odors that almost made Ibraha dizzy with nausea.

"These are all my medicines and cures for healing my people," he explained to Ibraha, waving his arms about.

The shaman's sleeping place was a pile of sweet smelling cedar brush covered with a tanned mooseskin. In the center of the dirt floor, a pile of stones formed a fire pit which still glowed with a few embers. On the floor beside the crude bed, a bearskin had been placed with the still-attached head facing east.

"You have proven yourself to be a fine warrior. Our squaw sachem has spoken of how you protected her from the vilest treachery of Henry Kendall and his kind; how you brought her back from near death from the big ocean storm. She has told us of your kindness and consideration for her comfort during her long days on the ocean."

"I loved her even then, Keeper-of-the-Faith."

"You must have a clan name. I have heard of your skill hunting the whales, so your turtle name will be Whale Hunter."

"I will be proud to have that name. The whale is a beast I admire greatly."

"With this name, my son, you will be a member of the turtle clan of the Wampanoag tribe of the Algonquin nation. I have something else to tell you that is most important to your future life."

The Keeper-of-the-Faith stood and placed a firm hand on Ibraha's shoulder. When he spoke, Ibraha recognized a solemnity in his next words.

"Any issue you may have will belong to the

Wampanoag tribe. The line of heritage extends from the child's mother, not the father. Can you be content with such a ruling?"

Ibraha's answer came without hesitation, and was firm and clear. "I love Akayna as my life. I know life for me would be nothing without her. And her blood will be mixed with my blood and that of my father's that reaches back to the kings of Africa." He held his head erect and proud as he spoke. "I bring a strong heritage from Africa to this new world. My father and forefathers would have me come with nothing less."

"That is good. Then we shall have the ceremony soon. There will be two ceremonies in one. The first will be to make you a clan member and the second will be the joining of you and our squaw sachem. One thing more, Ibraha. It is our custom for the man to present a gift to his woman. Do you have something of value?"

Ibraha reached around his neck and untied a leather thong. From a small pouch, he extracted a piece of cloth about two inches square. He unwrapped the cloth to reveal a gold ring inlaid with lapis lazuli. "My father was a lapidary in the old world," he told the Keeper-of-the-Faith. "He made this ring and gave it to my mother when he married her. She wore it until the day she died. I was only a small boy of ten when she called me to her death bed and gave it to me. It is all I have that remains of my parents. Will it do?"

The Keeper closed his fingers around the ring. "It is something that you love, therefore it is the perfect gift. I will present it to the squaw sachem in your name. It will be my honor." The shaman reached for his *calumet* beneath his mantle and filled the bowl with tobacco from his otterskin pouch. He had made a tobacco blend of smooth sumac leaves, sweet fern, crushed dogwood leaves and cardinal flower. Mixed with the shredded tobacco leaves, it made a satisfying smoke. He lit the pipe, and after taking several drafts, handed the pipe to Ibraha, who did the same.

As the smoke of the tobacco floated around their heads, a comfortable silence bound the two men as they sat on their stools and passed the smoking pipe back and forth.

Finally, the shaman cleared his throat. "It is not an easy path you have chosen, Whale Hunter," he said. "I fear for the future of us all, but especially for you two young people. I will ask the Great Spirit, *Kautantowwit*, god of the southwest winds, our greatest and most beloved god, to watch over you both. Now," he rose briskly to his feet and tucked his now-cooled pipe under his mantle, "I must prepare for the ceremonies. Do not eat or drink until my return. Do not leave this *wetu*. I will return for you when all is ready."

• • •

When the shaman came back to his *wetu* where Ibraha waited, he quickly raised his hand in a warning. "Do not speak until I tell you to do so. When you speak again, it will be as a member of our tribe. Now we must go to the steam bath for purification."

Other warriors who were to be Ibraha's honor guard waited for him in a large *wetu* that had been erected solely for the purpose. The men sat on stools around a fire pit with large stones that had been heated on it. Each stone was plunged into a bucket of wood that was charred hollow inside. Steam from the buckets filled the room, as the men's naked bodies glistened with the mixture of bear grease and perspiration. After a half hour, Ibraha, who was now being called Whale Hunter, was led to the stream that fed into the swamp. The cold water took his breath away, but he maintained a stoic silence. It was, he knew, an important ritual; an initiation that he had to endure. Finally, he felt, he was going to be one of these people. He had cast his lot with theirs.

One warrior, who he recognized as Yellow Bear, smiled wordlessly as he handed Ibraha a cloth made of coarse hemp with which to dry himself. Ibraha smiled, too.

Back inside the shaman's *wetu*, new, clean clothing had been laid out for Ibraha on the shaman's bed. There was a mooseskin robe of white, embroidered with figures of animals in red and violet. Along the hemline were threads of blue to simulate the ocean.

After Ibraha was dressed, Yellow Bear took a sharp stone and shaved his head on each side, leaving a strip of his curly black hair about one and one half inches wide from the front to back. He was given leggings of deerskin, and new moccasins were provided as well. Deer bristles that had been dyed red were tied to the strip of hair that had been made lustrous with bear grease. A band of beaded wampum was tied around Ibraha's forehead. He was beginning to feel more and more as if he belonged to these people, especially after Yellow Bear said, "Whale Hunter, you are fine man. Welcome to turtle clan."

Remembering the shaman's warning not to speak, Ibraha bowed and gave Yellow Bear a huge, wide grin. Then he was led into the large ceremonial long house.

Men, women and children, the whole tribe it seemed, sat in silent rows as the procession of the Keeper-of-the-Faith, Ibraha and his honor guard came forward.

There was an expectation of something important about to happen in the air.

Ibraha glanced at the faces around him; row after row of unsmiling, somber faces that showed they cared deeply about the events about to take place.

When the Keeper-of-the-Faith raised his hand, there was complete silence. Not a breath could be heard. His voice rang clearly in the long house. His words were to change Ibraha.

"Hah! Now to each in this place
Come as the sun brings new light.
Hah! Be to each a new brother
As a turtle in this clan.
Hah! Bear the name Whale Hunter.
Grind to the earth the old!
Hah! Stand, Whale Hunter!"

Then the shaman placed a cape made of turkey feathers around Ibraha's shoulders and led him to the center of the room. From the other side of the room, people standing in the doorway parted to make an aisle. Akayna, dressed in a white deerskin robe, and wearing her wampum belt of authority, came into the center of the room to face Ibraha. There were four young women with her as her attendants. They wore beige deerskin shifts and their new moccasins were white.

Akayna's hair fell down her back in a sheet of black silk. Her dark eyes were downcast demurely, and her face was flushed with emotion. With her rosy-tawny glow, Ibraha thought she looked like a radiant flower. His mind could scarcely believe that he was standing here in this place. *How has this come to be?* he wondered to himself. *Me, a seaman, whale hunter, great grandson of a West African, to be joining my life with the daughter of an Indian chief?*

The Keeper-of-the-Faith was speaking. Ibraha jerked himself from his reverie and heard the shaman ask his assistants to hand him two blankets. The Keeper gave one blanket to Akayna, who took it with her eyes still downcast. Then he presented the other blanket to Ibraha. "You both bring something to this union. It is your past, your present and your future." He turned to Akayna. "Do you, Akayna, desire to share with this man, Whale Hunter, all that you have and all that you will have? What is your answer?"

Akayna's voice was calm and clear. She looked up directly into the eyes of the man she loved, and in the expectant silence of the room, her answer could be heard in the farthest corners of the great lodge. "I will share all that I have and all I will ever have with this man, Whale Hunter," she said.

Ibraha wondered if his happiness would render him mute when his turn came. Could anyone see how nervous he was? He cleared his throat.

The Keeper turned to him. "Do you, Whale Hunter, desire to share all that you have and all that you will have with this woman, Akayna? You may speak."

Whale Hunter, Ibraha thought, *this new name speaks more of my old life than the one I now undertake. But I can live with it as long as this beautiful woman shares this new life with me.* He answered the shaman in a deep, resounding voice. No one could mistake his commitment to the woman who stood beside him. "I will share all that I have and all that I will ever have with this woman, Akayna."

The Keeper took the blankets from each of them. He unrolled each blanket, laid one on top of the other, and re-rolled them together. Then he joined the couple's hands. Ibraha saw his mother's ring on Akayna's finger. The Keeper then put the rolled blankets over their clasped hands. He turned the pair toward the assembly. "See the people who love you. Go forth in happiness, and may the Great Spirit blow only kind winds in your faces."

After this benediction, the radiant couple smiled at each other. As Ibraha bent to kiss Akayna, bedlam broke out.

From somewhere drums rolled, whistles and rattles sounded. All kinds of shouts, whoops and calls broke the silence as the happy couple walked through the throng. Ibraha could contain his own feelings of exuberance no longer. He raised his fist into the air and gave a loud whoop of joy.

The crowd laughed and joined him with whoops of their own. Then the men in the room broke into a song, a chorus of their own, which Akayna told Ibraha later were words of good luck and good fortune. Then the woman in their turn sang, almost like questions and answers, with each song ending in a loud yell. It was almost as if the wedding became a release from all the hardships the tribe had endured.

There was food, gifts, music and gaiety long into the fall evening. Young couples were moving into secluded areas in the campsite, evidently inspired by the wedding to seek liaisons of their own.

It was after midnight before the couple retired to Akayna's *wetu*. The charivari continued well into the night, but it did not disturb the lovers. They made love slowly and often during the night, rediscovering each time their delight in each other. Dawn found them still reaching for one another.

Akayna whispered to her husband, "Come, my dearest spouse; let us greet Mother Sun. Now you are one of us, a child of the first light." She grabbed his hand and, child-like, she led him out into the early dawn.

Frost had just started to appear, and the sparkling drops of dew made the grass and colorful fall leaves sparkle like iridescent crystal. Ibraha took several deep breaths — he could see his breath in the sharp air.

"Are you willing, *sannup,* husband mine?" Akayna asked shyly.

"Willing to do what?"

Akayna started off in a quick run and threw her garment off as she ran naked into the crisp cold water, laughing like a happy child. Ibraha tossed his mantle aside and joined Akayna as she splashed and frolicked in the stream. She splashed water in Ibraha's face as he swam to her; the water was warmer than he thought it would be.

He reached for Akayna, pulled her wet hair back from her face and held her naked body close to his own. As he felt the softness of her rounded breasts against his chest and her slender thighs touching his own, he could scarcely breathe. His emotions tightened in his throat. He kissed her eyes, her open lips and whispered hoarsely, "I will always follow you, my love, wherever you are. I love you."

CHAPTER TWENTY-FIVE

Theirs was a peaceful life. Living near the Great Swamp, away from the encroaching English, Akayna's tribe carried on their lives much as in the old days. Ibraha went out with the men to hunt and fish, and Akayna made their *wetu* into a comfortable retreat. She carried out her duties as squaw sachem — mediating disputes, and checking to see that a harvest of nuts, dried fruits and vegetables were set aside for the winter. She was also responsible for a census taking, and she recorded the names of the tribe's newborn on the wampum storytelling belt.

Their evenings were spent sharing the day's events. Akayna was anxious for Ibraha to fit into her life.

"Did you enjoy the hunt today, Whale Hunter?" she would ask.

"Well, I can't get used to the bow and arrow that the hunters use. I'd rather have my trusty harpoon. I could do better, I think."

"But Yellow Bear and the others say that you have true aim, even with the bow and arrow."

"Having to draw the bow and steady the arrow seems slow to me. With my harpoon and my arm, I have more speed and strength."

"Hmm," Akayna mused. "Could you make a harpoon, Whale Hunter?"

"Indeed, if we had the metal and the forge, I could do it."

"We can find those things for you. Then perhaps you can teach my warriors."

Ibraha really meant it when he told Akayna he would follow her wherever her path took her. But there was something about living in a small Indian village that began to bother him. The dusty paths of the village from *wetu* to *wetu*; the idle days spent with the men when they were not hunting or fishing, just sitting around smoking and talking while the women tended the fields and the children, began to bore him. It was not like the active life he had on the sea.

He found himself longing to be back on the ocean, feeling a decent ship under his feet, smelling the brisk salt air as the ship moved nimbly to perhaps a new and fascinating destination. And he was bothered by the promise he'd made to Alan Rosewood to return for the whale hunt. As a proud African from Guinea, he could not go back on his word. The more he thought about it, the more restless he became.

His restlessness had not gone unnoticed. One evening Ibraha pushed aside his half-empty plate. Akayna spoke perceptively, "My love, you're not happy, are you?" Before Ibraha could answer, she continued. "I can see it in your face. Life here is more different than you expected."

"Oh, Akayna," Ibraha protested, "you know I'm happy to be with you. You are my life..."

"But I don't think my life is enough for you. I've

seen your eyes going to the far horizon and I've felt your restless tossing and turning about in our cedar bark bed. If you are unhappy, husband mine, I will not force you to stay."

"Force me? Oh, Akayna, there is no need to talk like that? No one has 'forced' me. I'm here with you because I love you. You are the woman of my life." He reached for her and gathered her in his arms. He tilted her face toward his and bent to kiss her. "I love you," he murmured.

But Akayna thought, *how much does he really love me? Am I asking too much of him? Does a man feel less than a man if he follows a woman, even if she is a squaw sachem?*

She sighed deeply, and Ibraha's heart fell as he recognized her frustration. He continued to kiss her eyes, mouth, the soft spot in her slender neck, and then he led her to their bed. At least there they could meet each other's needs.

• • •

It was two days later that a runner came into the village with the breathless news that Alan Rosewood was ready to embark on the whale hunt, and he was asking for Ibraha. Some of the men in the village showed interest in such a new adventure, if Ibraha should decide to make the trip. It was the talk of the village.

Akayna agonized. She knew firsthand the depths of the sea, the sudden storms that could toss a ship almost into oblivion, no matter how skilled the seamen were.

There was one other thing on her mind. Ibraha did not know she carried his child. It had been two months since she had seen her moonflow. She had decided that she would not influence Ibraha's decision by telling him. If he decided to go on this hunt, she would keep silent.

The excitement of some of the other men in the village could hardly be contained. Yellow Bear had approached Ibraha several times. "Will you go with the English sailor, Whale Hunter?"

Ibraha later broached the subject to Akayna, as she sat repairing a hemp basket. When he entered the *wetu,* his heart leaped with joy when he saw her bent over her work. Now that she was a married woman, she wore her hair in a single braid. Often she would coil it crown-like on the top of her head. The fall days were becoming shorter and the sun was not as strong as it was in the summer, so her skin was becoming less ruddy and showed more gold in its hue. As he looked at her, Ibraha thought, *how lucky I am to share my life with this wonderful woman. She is like a wood nymph, a goddess, in my heart. I never want to hurt her, but I must speak.*

"Akayna, my beloved..."

His young wife smiled as he approached and sat close to her.

"Yes, Whale Hunter."

"I've decided that I must honor my promise to help Alan Rosewood in his whale hunt. I must return to Monset."

He looked tenderly at the woman who was now his wife. A mere slip of a girl no longer, she had blossomed into a stunningly beautiful woman. Her skin was so soft, his fingers tingled with the memory of touching it. Her face glowed warmly, its golden, tawny coloring enhanced by the feathery dark lashes that framed her sable-brown eyes. Glossy black hair, glorious in its thickness and silky sheen, shaped her face into a portrait of such breathtaking beauty that Ibraha could hardly believe this wondrous creature was his. Never had he known a woman who so touched him that every fiber of his body seemed to yearn for her. And his joy in knowing that she returned his love made it even more important that he love and protect her at all costs.

He moaned inwardly at the profusion of thoughts warring for prominence in his mind. It would be like tearing out his heart to leave her, but how else could he accomplish what needed to be done? How could he leave behind the nights of sensual lovemaking, the tantalizing warmth of her exquisite body next to his? How could he leave those wild, untamed moments when he kissed and savored the honeyed sweetness of her full round breasts with the erotic buds that flowered when he tasted them with his searching tongue? As he looked at her, he felt his determination to leave begin to weaken; his strong desire was to take her at that very moment, scoop her into his hungry, aching arms and seek relief from the intensity of the longing for her that was rising, unbidden, from within him.

Her dark, luminous eyes were on him now, as if searching his face for denial of his intent. She watched him stand and move to the door of the *wetu*. If he turned his back to her, it would almost be a symbol of his parting. The sight of his lithe, yet manly, body thrilled her. It was *his* strong arms that would shield her from harm, *his* fierce heart that thudded against hers in their most intimate moments of joy. How could she bear to let him go? If he did, she would have no one. Again, she would be a lonely squaw sachem. She felt herself melt under his scrutiny. This tall, stalwart, ebony man who did not exist for her six months ago was now the most central person in her life. Since that warm sunny day in Funchal, this man, this understanding being, had affected her like no one else. But this talk of leaving to hunt whales — wasn't *she* the squaw sachem, the leader of her people? Her thoughts became muddled, and she forgot her resolve to hold her tongue. When she spoke, the words sounded strange to her as they fell from her lips, and she wanted to call them back.

"I forbid it," she spoke slowly. I forbid you to leave. You cannot."

Ibraha's eyes widened in surprise as if to check the validity of Akayna's statement. He laughed aloud. "Forbid me? Oh, my dearest Akayna, you can't mean that."

"Oh, but I do. *I'm* the leader of the turtle clan of the Wamponoags. How will it look to my people if even my husband defies me to do what he wants?"

It was almost as if the words could not stay in her mouth. Her eyes smoldered with the intensity of her anger as she continued to speak. "*I* am the squaw sachem! *I* am the leader of these people. *I* bear their burdens as well as my own and *I* say you will not go with the Englishman! You cannot disobey me!"

Akayna did not know where her words came from. She could have bitten her tongue to bring them back, but they lay in the air like a miasmic fog that obscured them from one another.

Ibraha saw the fire in Akayna's eyes. Even in her anger he loved her, and he wanted nothing more than to take her in his arms and make everything perfect. But she had thrown down a challenge and he knew he had to answer. His voice was quiet and deliberate, as if somehow he could bring calm to this turbulent moment.

"Akayna, I would give my life for you. But you know that. This I must tell you, my dear wife. There has been in my life only one other person that I loved and adored as much as I love you, and that was my beloved mother. But as a proud Susu man, and her son, I would not have allowed my own mother to tell me what I could or couldn't do. I promised Alan Rosewood to help him with his whale hunt, and I will honor that promise. He helped me... when I didn't even know if I'd ever see you again..."

"If you go," she interrupted him, her body rigid and tense as she stood before him, "if you go, do not come back. I will divorce you. I will."

She was shaken when she saw Ibraha's cold, dark, unrelieving stare. She knew then that she had angered him. Her insides quivered. Had she gone too far; pushed too hard to have her own way?

She threw her shoulders back and braced herself for Ibraha's response. She met his glare with her own look of stony resentment. Between them, the fog of distrust was becoming an icy wall.

Ibraha's words came slow and measured, as if correcting a recalcitrant child. "But you won't," he said softly. Then he reached for her.

She tried to resist, to hold herself tense and unyielding, but she did not have the strength. Trembling with anger toward herself for being bound by the love she had for her husband, her anger at Ibraha for daring to leave her was still overwhelming. She wanted to flee from his embrace, but she knew more than anything she wanted his arms around her. His very nearness weakened her as she responded to his touch.

His next words flowed over her like a soft, cleansing spring breeze. "A short time ago, you were a young girl, living here with your family. But you have traveled to the other side of this world, and you have come to know as well as anyone the vastness of it. You *cannot* forbid me, my wife. I would be less than a suitable husband if I didn't at least try to do what I think is right. My ancestors go back to a long line of Susu men whose firm belief was to protect what belonged to them at all costs, and," he added, "you belong to me."

He looked into her eyes. She saw love and caring in his face. His warmth and tenderness reached out to her as he bent his head to kiss her. She welcomed his firm lips on hers with a hunger she didn't know she had. Ibraha's tongue sought the sweetness of her mouth as he reached beneath her linen shift to caress her. Akayna moaned, as they both fell back onto the soft, fur-covered bed.

"I'm sorry Whale Hunter, Ibraha," she murmured. "When I am in your arms, I'm all that I want to be, your wife." Tears flooded her eyes as she looked at the loving face of the man she had come to love and trust. Through the curtain of tears she saw his strong, dark head; the curly shaft of black hair that ennobled his looks as it grew from his forehead to the nape of his neck. His black eyebrows, straight and unwavering, shadowed his obsidian eyes with a masculinity that could not be denied. Beneath her hands she could feel the marble-smooth, firm muscles of his arms as she passed her fingers over his satin-like ebony skin. The touch tingled her fingers with excitement, and she saw responding passion flame in Ibraha's eyes. Perhaps he would leave her, perhaps she would have to suffer loneliness again, but there was one thing she knew. She loved this gentle African whose heart beat so strongly beneath her searching hands.

And he loved her. His lips on hers were like liquid fire, and she savored the sensation like a greedy child. Ibraha's fingers continued their exploration. Frantic, neither could wait as they tore away the simple garments that covered their bodies. Now it was Ibraha who moaned as he sought and tasted every part of her soft, young body. The heat of his lips and tongue on her eyes, neck, the valley between her breasts, and her rounded abdomen, sent rippling sensations through her body. And when the tantalizing, sweet sensation reached the intriguing regions between her petal soft thighs, Akayna whimpered with delirious joy.

She clung to him and pulled his face to hers as the rapture enveloped them. Her lithe legs enveloped his waist, and she wrapped her arms around his neck, forcing his mouth once more upon hers, seeking almost to drain his love from him. She writhed beneath his taut body to fit herself into the curves and planes of her husband, so that their oneness could not be separated. Ibraha's response was powerful and sure. Their bodies fused, rising to a towering crest of fulfillment as they both reached the pinnacle of sensual completion. Exhausted, they held each other close.

As they grew quiet, their breathing slowed, the silvery sheen of perspiration glowed on their bodies, and Akayna stroked the rock-hard shoulder muscles of her husband as he lay in her arms. Silent tears rolled down her cheeks. She wanted him to stay, not ever leave her, but this night would be forever in her memory. She knew she had to relent. She couldn't keep her husband if he wanted to leave. He did not know that she carried his child. She would let him go, unencumbered, to do what he thought was right. She realized now that she loved him more than ever, because this man would defy all odds, even her, to do what he believed in.

She felt his warm soft breath flutter in her ear as his loving face lay close to hers. "You are my heart, *sannup,* husband mine," she whispered softly. "I will always love only you." *Please, Great Spirit, Kautantowwit, give him strong winds, safe seas and a quick return to my arms,* she prayed.

• • •

Ibraha found Yellow Bear and some of the other young men playing a game in a large, cleared field. Dirt had replaced the grass that had once grown there, and the playing field was smooth and free of rocks and impediments. A dirt trough, about a foot wide, had been formed down the center of the field, about seventy-five yards long.

As Ibraha stood on the sidelines, he watched as Yellow Bear and his team of five warriors challenged Leaping Wolf and his five men. Each man had his own stick about five feet long. At the end of each stick there was a slight bulge that looked like a snake's head. The object of the game was to slide the stick down the dirt trough. The team that slid their dirt-snakes the farthest was the winner.

Several young women were at the playing field, vigorously cheering on their team with yelling, screaming, and jumping up and down on the sidelines.

Some of the men, although quite slender, had well-defined arms and shoulders. They would run in a brisk manner toward the edge of the trough, give a mighty groan, and slide the dirt-snakes as far as possible. Ibraha admired their muscular strength.

When Yellow Bear noticed Ibraha, he waved to him. "Come, Whale Hunter! Try you luck with the dirt-snake! Here, use mine."

"I'd like to, Yellow Bear. Looks like fun, but I want to talk about something more serious."

Yellow Bear wiped the perspiration from his dripping face and dried his hands on his loin cloth. He was all attention. "Yes, Whale Hunter, have you decided?"

• • •

When Jocko growled, Alan Rosewood reached for his gun. "Yes laddie, what is it? Strangers?" He peered over the wooden railing of the *Mighty Maiden* and relaxed. "'Tis ye, Ibraha, ye've come back."

"As I said I would. And I have brought a crew with me."

Alan grinned broadly when he saw the group of men standing with Ibraha on the beach.

"Gor' blimy, that's a bit o' all right! Ye came! Was thinkin' to meself t'other day, the 'drifters' will be offshore enny day now, they'll be movin' by here southward to their breedin' grounds. But bein' a whalin' man, ye know all 'bout that, eh?"

"Pretty much," Ibraha offered.

"Wal, don' stan' there jawin'... ye 'n' yer crew climb aboard. We'll make a deal 'n' seal it wi' a drink."

"Thanks, sir, but no drinks. We must have a deal, though," Ibraha responded as he, Yellow Bear, Leaping Wolf, and the others clambered aboard, somewhat tentatively. Some of the young warriors had never been on so large a ship as the *Mighty Maiden*.

"It is my understanding that any whales we bring in,

the government in England will demand a portion...,"
Ibraha began.

"Aye," Rosewood interrupted, "'n' the town claims another portion, which leaves a third fer us. What do ye think, Ibraha? Will that do; kin we strike a deal?"

"Have you seen many 'drifters' about, Alan? How much will your ship's hold take in?" Ibraha said before answering Rosewood's question.

"Look, ah've plenty of room for the processin' of at leas' four whales, mebbe five, dependin' on the size."

"A good-sized 'right' whale should bring at least four thousand pounds in English currency. If we take in four or five animals, that's sixteen to twenty thousand pounds all told," Ibraha suggested.

"Aye, yer right," Rosewood answered.

Ibraha extended his hand and the Englishman grasped it firmly.

"Almost didn' know ye' wi' yer new hair cut 'n' all, Ibraha. Gone over to the tribe, hev' ye?"

"Indeed, Alan, I've cast my lot with these people. I've married their squaw sachem. But I promised to help you and I'm here."

Rosewood spat over the side of the ship, as the Indian warriors looked from one man to the other as the conversation went back and forth.

He rubbed his hands in glee. "Did ye bring any tools wi' ye?"

"We have spear-throwing weights, bone spear points, ball-headed clubs, hatchets and many sharp knives for flensing, stripping the blubber from the whales," Ibraha told him. "And we brought a good supply of bows, arrows, prickers, and spikes on short poles for handling the cut up blubber."

"Good, good," Rosewood effused, he was so excited at the prospect of the hunt. "Ah'm not a man to be ill-prepared meself, me friend. Ah've been accumulatin' since ye left 'gainst the day ye'd be back. Below deck o' the *Mighty Maiden* there's flensin' hooks, knives, rope, harpoons, 'n' ah've even got two big try-pots for refinin' the blubber. Tomorry, we'll start out firs' light ter see if we kin raise a few whales!"

CHAPTER TWENTY-SIX

Ibraha thought of his uncle and his days whaling off the coast of Spain and northwest Africa. As a boy, he had soon learned that a whaling ship was a busy place to be, especially when a whale was spotted.

He stood on the deck of the *Mighty Maiden* with Yellow Bear, and wondered if the young Indians would be able to master whale hunting. Most of their hunting had been on land, for bear and moose. But he was sure they would be equal to the task once they were shown how to do the work.

As the *Mighty Maiden* sailed down the eastern coast for a gam of whales, most of the warriors had taken readily to the life at sea. A few were seasick, but the majority learned the art of seamanship under the tutelage of Rosewood and Ibraha. The Englishman was impressed.

"By gor, Ibraha, they take to the sea like they was bloody born to it," he told Ibraha.

"Aye," Ibraha answered with unmistakable pride, "I have found them eager to learn and they do it quickly. They are good men."

A few days later, they found what they had been

searching for. They had reached the feeding grounds of some "drift" whales. In the bustle of taking the whales, preparing the blubber, "trying-out" and storing the oil in barrels, there was scarcely time to think. In the evening when the men were at last able to rest, some worked at scrimshaw, etched scenes and pictures on whales' teeth; others played a needle and bone game in which they tried to catch threaded bones on a needle, and others wagered on a disc game where they would bet which colored side of the disc would show when the disc was thrown. Ibraha would stand most often at the wheel of the *Sea Maiden*, his thoughts on his wife, Akayna.

As he stood looking out over the ocean, her lovely face would swim into his mind. He could see her dark sooty eyes, her firm chin and her velvety, tawny skin. She was so beautiful and he loved her so. Not only because of her beauty, but also for her single-minded willingness to follow the path her tribe had set for her. She would not falter from the task of squaw sachem, despite the cost. He admired the pride she had in herself and in her people. *Living is sharing,* he thought. Would Akayna see his pride in himself, and would the love they shared be enough to sustain each other's pride?

• • •

It had been many moons since Ibraha sailed away from his wife. Akayna went about her daily duties, as usual. Each day brought new problems to solve for the members of her tribe. So far, the settlers had upheld the treaty for the most part, but they were steadily moving closer to the tribe's encampment. Twice, the Keeper-of-the-Faith had returned to Governor General Sheridan's office with messages from his squaw sachem regarding encroachment incidents.

Winter had set in, and was particularly harsh. Several of the children had contracted a virus, which kept the Keeper-of-the-Faith moving from *wetu* to *wetu* to administer herbs and medicines.

In the bright of day, and with all her activities as squaw sachem, Akayna could almost bury the emptiness she felt. But in the stillness of the long nights, loneliness engulfed her. She was haunted by memories of her beloved husband. Oh, how she missed him.

Tonight, as Akayna lay awake in her *wetu,* her thoughts returned to the happiness they had shared and her fears resurfaced. She knew all too well the dangers of the sea. She had returned to her homeland only to lose her beloved father. Was she destined to lose the man who gave her life its meaning, too?

Ibraha had spent his life on the sea. It was what he knew and loved. It was what had brought them together. Did she expect too much to believe he could be content with life as a member of the turtle clan? Did her love for him blind her to his needs? Would things be different if she had not forbad him to leave?

So many questions rambled through Akayna's mind, as she tossed and turned upon the bed they had shared. "My Ibraha, my Whale Hunter," she moaned into the silence.

The child within her was restless, as though it, too, feared for the father who did not know of its existence. Would he ever know? What difficulties would this "different" child suffer without the strength of its father's protection?

Akayna gently stroked her swollen belly until her unborn child finally settled into a peaceful rest. As streaks of early sunlight drifted through her *wetu,* she, too, floated off to sleep.

• • •

Ibraha remembered that not too long ago he had vowed to leave whale hunting. *"I love Akayna as my life. She rules it, and I know life for me would be nothing without her."* His words came back to him.

Why, then, was he here on this ship when his whole body ached to be with the woman he loved. He knew now, on this deep, dark ocean, that whatever the cost, whatever happened, his life, his future, was entwined with hers. Life on the sea had taught him that precarious situations and hazards were ever present, like the storm at Cape Hatteras that had cost the lives of two of the Indians. It wasn't worth it. Never again would he take another risk on the sea. When he returned to Akayna this time, he would never leave her again.

Oh, Akayna, my precious love, he thought, *I want you always in my life. Be proud of me and love me. All I can give you is what I am, a whale hunter who yearns for your love.*

He sighed and turned his attention to the dark, unrelenting waters as the *Mighty Maiden* plowed its way back to the Cape waters. *I'm coming back, my love,* Ibraha breathed silently, as he turned the wheel. The ship gave a steep plunge into the water as she headed into the wind and home.

CHAPTER TWENTY-SEVEN

When the *Mighty Maiden* came into Succonesset, the harbor "where black clams were found," she moved very slowly. Her hold was full of barrels of whale oil and her decks were piled high with bundles of baleen.

The ship had been gone nearly five months, three months longer than Ibraha had calculated. It was *Squocheekeewush,* the month of February, when "the sun begins to warm the frozen earth." As soon as Alan Rosewood dropped anchor, most of the Indians dashed for their canoes to get ashore. They were anxious to feel solid Mother Earth beneath their feet again. Several vowed never again to go away on the big sea. They were the ones plagued by seasickness, but there were others who enjoyed the excitement and the hunt of the large sea animals that they had helped pursue and capture.

Ibraha and Yellow Bear stayed on board to oversee the cargo until Alan Rosewood, who went off in one of the first canoes, could return with a government official to certify the ship and its cargo.

Within a couple of hours, Alan Rosewood was back with the officials, who certified the cargo and returned to Monset. "Well, Ibraha!" he grinned at the tall African he had come to admire and respect, "due to yer skill 'n' that o' yer men, we've done handsomely. Hev' two thousand pounds ter giv' ye right out now, 'n' ah will be leavin' the dust o' this godfersaken place, jes' as soon as ah kin scare up a crew to get back to merry ol' England!"

"I'm glad it was a good hunt, Alan, in spite of the fact that it took longer than we expected. But you never know when or where the whales will be. Who would have thought we would end up following the whales all the way to Cape Hatteras?"

"Yes," Rosewood answered soberly, "an' I'm sorry about that. Runnin' into that storm that took two of yer men; that was the bad part. Ye'll tell their families they were brave men?"

"I surely will, and we'll share the money with their families. Now, Alan, you say you're returning to England soon?"

"Aye, the sooner the better. Ah know bad times are comin', but ter git back to me missus 'n' live out me old days in me small garden, 'tis all ah'm askin' from life."

Alan Rosewood, Ibraha, and Yellow Bear, with the help of a few Indians still on board, eased the *Mighty Maiden* into a cove where she would be safe until unloaded.

Ibraha shook hands with Rosewood and he, Yellow Bear, and the rest of the men set out across the Great Swamp for home.

When they arrived that night, great fires were burning to greet them. Everyone was feasting and dancing; the excitement was almost palpable.

Ibraha was glad Akayna was not in the joyous crowd. He wanted their coming together to be private. He walked up the path to their *wetu*. The skin flap was open, and he stepped inside. Quickly his eyes adjusted to the dim light from the everlit center fire. He drew a deep breath and looked around. Then he saw her. She was sitting on her bearskin brush pile, the simple bed that they had come together on.

"Akayna," Ibraha breathed.

She looked at him, stood up and opened her arms to receive him. Her hair was loose and flowing around her shoulders; she knew he wanted it that way. She extended her arms and clasped them around his neck as he picked her up and swung her from the dirt floor.

"Whale Hunter, oh Ibraha, you are really here at last!"

"Of course, my love, I'm here. I will never leave you again. His kisses rained on her face, eyebrows, nose, throat and lips. He breathed heavily and groaned, "Do you know how much I love you?"

"Enough to be with me always?" she volunteered as she kissed him back in return.

"Always, always and forever, my beautiful Akayna, my squaw sachem."

He carried her back to the bed and slowly, almost ritualistically, removed her simple clothing. First he took off her moccasins, and he kissed the soles of her feet. Then her leggings, and he caressed each tawny leg with his lips. He loosened the drawstring of her shift and pulled it down over her bare shoulders. The loveliness of her rounded breasts took his breath away, and he gently lay his face down on them.

Akayna cradled his head on her bosom as tears of welcome seeped silently from under her eyelids. She whispered to herself, *Thank you, kind Great Spirit, for returning my beloved husband to me.*

Ibraha raised his head to her face, and felt the flowing tears from Akayna's closed eyelids. "Don't cry my sweet, I'm here, I'm here," he soothed.

He rose and quickly stripped off his breeches and his shirt, then gently pulled Akayna's deerskin shift from her body. In the dim light he had not noticed her rounded belly, but when he touched her stomach, his hand sprang back as he felt a slight quiver of movement beneath his hand.

Momentarily stunned, Ibraha's movement froze. Could this be? When he was finally able to speak, his voice was hoarse with emotion. "Akayna, my beloved one. You are carrying our child! I never dreamed... oh, Akayna, can you forgive me for leaving you for so long? I didn't know..." his voice choked, as he kissed her softly parted lips.

"I did not want to tell you when you left, my husband, because I felt it would be an unfair way to hold you when you had made up your mind."

"So you did not tell me. I'm not sure I would have gone if I had known. You are well?" he inquired.

"I am well, and I am happy now," she murmured into his chest as he stroked his long, firm fingers over her abdomen. His touch was soothing and loving, and Akayna sighed deeply. A feeling of security came that she thought she'd never have again. Not since she was a little girl living in her parents' *wetu,* spoiled and indulged by all the people of the tribe, had she felt so safe. Ever since the death of Ella Gardner, her life had been in turmoil. Now, tonight, lying in the arms of her strong, ebony husband, she again quietly gave thanks.

"My sweet one," Ibraha whispered, caressing her

eyes, cheeks and mouth with soft kisses. He could hardly believe he was here in their *wetu* and his beloved wife was in his arms. It had been so long. In deep gratitude, he nestled his head on her breasts as he tried to comprehend how close he had come to losing... everything. With gentle love, he kissed Akayna again and again, as if afraid of letting her go.

This is where I want to be, he thought, *not on the sea.* The ocean took lives at will. He was fortunate they had not all perished at Cape Hatteras. The risk of that life was even more valueless because it took him from the woman he loved. And wonder of wonders, he would be a father soon. Whatever may come, he was forever tied to this woman. He knew that now. This life, this culture, this future was to be theirs together.

Silence filled the small space within the *wetu* as Ibraha continued to hold Akayna. Across the back of his neck he could feel the cool February air as it drifted through the smoke hole of the animal hide roof.

Akayna heard a robin chirp as it hopped along the ground outside. She heard tree peepers signal their trilling calls. She remembered that *Sequanakeeswuch* had just begun. It was the time for herring to leave the ocean waters of the Cape and run upstream to spawn, a time for new life. Inwardly she prayed, *may this new spring bring us peace and happiness.*

Ibraha and Akayna kissed again and again, their mouths exploring and claiming each others with an intensity they both shared. Memories of the past year were behind them. From Africa's dusty coast of Guinea to the sparkling blue waters of Torremolinos, to the welcoming arm of the Cape, Ibraha had found an unbelievable destiny in the captivating arms of Akayna, the daughter of an Indian sachem. Banished from the safety of her home and loved ones, destiny had taken Akayna, squaw sachem, to the strange shores of foreign lands and back again, to find a love that surpassed any she had ever known. Never could they have known that fateful day in Funchal that they would love each other. But they knew this day that they would love each other as long as they lived.

THE END

ACKNOWLEDGEMENTS

My sincere thanks are due Ann Tanneyhill, chairperson of the Mashpee Historical Commission and the staff of the Mashpee Archives, Mashpee, Massachusetts, for their immeasurable assistance in my research of the Wamponoags of Cape Cod. Thanks to Tall Oak, a surviving Wamponoag, who told me about Kautantowwit, the Great Spirit.

Both the New Bedford Whaling Museum on Johnny-Cake Hill, New Bedford, Massachusetts and the Kendall Whaling Museum in Sharon, Massachusetts, gave me help in learning about the whaling industry. My appreciation is extended to all who were so kind to me.